"Ready to start talking?

Vivianne sighed. "I don't suppose I have much of a choice."

"Not really, no."

"I'm Vivi Donner, by the way."

Cam rolled the name around his mind, could easily imagine himself whispering it as he kissed her, painting it on her skin as he tongued her. Sighing it as he slid into her hot, wet warmth. Cam gave himself a mental punch to the temple.

Yeah, he was still attracted to her, but so what?

He cursed himself for not being able to forget about her—and he cursed her for dropping back into his life, for making him yearn and burn. He'd never forgotten her and he hated her for that. This brown-eyed woman made him feel like his world was shifting, that something was changing.

Vivi's reappearance in his life was going to rock him to the soles of his feet.

"Why am I your emergency contact, Vivianne?"

Whatever color was left in Vivi's face drained away.

"I have a daughter, Clementine. She's two years old...and you are her father."

* * *

That Night in Texas is part of the Texas Cattleman's Club: Houston series.

Dear Reader,

A storm has slammed Houston, and it's chaotic. The Texas Cattleman's Club is opening in Houston, and two families with a complicated history are vying for control of the club. But there is someone else who wants revenge on the Perry and Currin clans…

Camden McNeal and Vivi Donner slept together three years ago and parted without exchanging contact details. They've both come a long way in a short time. Cam is now a venture capitalist and Vivi is an executive chef and mom to Cam's daughter, Clem.

After recognizing Cam in her restaurant, Vivi toyed with telling Cam about Clem, but the fear that he would take control of her and Clem's lives made her hesitate. But in case something happened to her, she named Cam as Clem's father in her will and as her emergency contact.

And then something awful did happen and suddenly, in the aftermath of the storm, Cam is faced with the woman he could never forget and the child he never knew he fathered. Can Cam and Vivi, with all their baggage and stubbornness, find love and the family they both need?

Read on to find out!

Happy reading,

Joss

Connect with me at www.josswoodbooks.com

Twitter: @josswoodbooks

Facebook: Joss Wood Author

JOSS WOOD

THAT NIGHT IN TEXAS

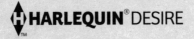

Rebecca Crowley—amazing writer and Jozi survivor— thanks for sharing Houston with me. And for introducing me to Mexican beer, Colombian food and pumping your own gas. It'll be a trip I'll always remember.

Nkosi Sikelel' iAfrika

Special thanks and acknowledgment are given to Joss Wood for her contribution to the Texas Cattleman's Club: Houston miniseries.

ISBN-13: 978-1-335-60361-6

That Night in Texas

Copyright © 2019 by Harlequin Books S.A.

Recycling programs for this product may not exist in your area.

Printed in U.S.A.

www.Harlequin.com

Joss Wood loves books and traveling—especially to the wild places of Southern Africa and, well, anywhere. She's a wife, a mom to two teenagers and slave to two cats. After a career in local economic development, she now writes full-time. Joss is a member of Romance Writers of America and Romance Writers of South Africa.

Books by Joss Wood

Harlequin Desire

The Ballantyne Billionaires

His Ex's Well-Kept Secret
One Night to Forever
The CEO's Nanny Affair
Little Secrets: Unexpectedly Pregnant

Love in Boston

Friendship on Fire
Hot Christmas Kisses
The Rival's Heir

Texas Cattleman's Club: Bachelor Auction

Lone Star Reunion

Visit her Author Profile page at Harlequin.com, or josswoodbooks.com, for more titles.

You can find Joss Wood on Facebook, along with other Harlequin Desire authors, at Facebook.com/harlequindesireauthors!

One

Vivi Donner gripped her steering wheel and leaned forward, hoping that the extra couple of inches would help her see better through the gray, dense fog. It was another awful day after a string of terrible days, and like the rest of the residents of Houston, Texas, she felt both battered and shattered. After the storm that had led to devastating flooding, a blast of sunshine would help. But a clear day would also force Houston to face the destruction that had been caused and to take stock of the extensive damage to homes and buildings. Vivi jerked her eyes off to the side and the fog cleared just enough for her to see the piles of debris, broken branches and ruined furniture on the sidewalks.

Thank God her house, and that of Clem's sitter,

Charlie, was undamaged. The same couldn't be said for The Rollin' Smoke, the famed barbecue restaurant where she worked as head chef.

According to Joe, the owner and her mentor, her beautiful, newly updated kitchen was ruined. The renovations to the restaurant had been finished just six weeks ago, and the new floor, booths, tables and chairs were all wrecked, as well. Garbage and debris still covered the floor, and all hands, including hers, were needed on deck.

As the head chef who answered only to Joe, she could wait until her staff did the heavy lifting and cleaning before she returned, but she wasn't a prima donna. How could she be? She'd worked her way up the ladder at the restaurant—albeit in record time—from dishwasher to head chef, but she still knew how to get her hands dirty.

Joe's name might be on the deeds to the eatery but The Rollin' Smoke was hers, dammit, and Vivi wanted to be there to pick it up and dry it off.

Seeing that the road ahead was closed, Vivi turned down a side road. The fog was thicker here, and her visibility was rapidly decreasing. If it got much worse, she'd have to stop and wait it out, but that could take hours. Where was that damn sun? She lifted one hand from the steering wheel and rubbed her hand on her soft denims, trying to wipe away the perspiration. God, this was scary.

The ringing of her phone had her butt lifting two

inches off her seat. Fumbling, she hit the screen to answer the call. "God, Joe, you scared me!"

"Are you in the car? Please tell me you're not driving!" Joe's voice rose in panic.

"Actually, I'm crawling along." That way, nothing bad could happen.

"Turn around, go back home."

Vivi fought the urge to do exactly that. She wanted to pick up Clem and take her back to their house, climb into bed and pull the covers over their heads and hide out from the world. But she'd done that for the first quarter century of her life and she refused to live like that again. Life was for living, dammit, and part of that living was accepting the good with the bad.

Having Clem and being her mom was not just good but stupendously awesome. On the flip side, a devastating storm and the resulting flood was bad— *terrible*—but it had happened, and she had to deal with it.

"I have a job to do and a restaurant to clean up so that our lives can return to normal as soon as possible. A little destruction won't stop the ravenous appetites of Houston meat eaters," Vivi told Joe, ignoring the sense that she was standing on a precipice. She had a feeling that nothing would ever be the same again.

Vivi shivered as a cold chill ran up and down her spine. Her mom would've said that a devil was dancing on her spine, but Vivi shook that thought away. Her mom's superstitions and beliefs, a curious mix of religion and craziness, no longer had a place in her life.

She was just freaked out by the fog, the lack of streetlights, the whistling wind and the piles of debris she occasionally caught a glimpse of in her weak headlights. They all contributed to the spooky atmosphere.

"Just be careful, please," Joe begged her before disconnecting the call.

Another shiver raised the hair on her arms and Vivi swore. Dropping her eyes, she looked down and located the temperature controls. She punched the button to warm the interior of the car. It was hot and humid outside, but her body had other ideas.

Grateful for the blast of warm air, Vivi checked her rearview mirror and saw a cop car on her tail, blue lights flashing. Vivi scanned the road ahead of her, cursing when she realized there was nowhere to pull over. He was close to her tail and she saw, in her rearview mirror, big hands fly up in obvious frustration. He needed to be somewhere else and she was in his way. Her only option was to speed up and hope a spot would soon appear where she could pull over.

Vivi flexed her fingers and took a deep breath. And as soon as she accelerated she saw the spooky outline of a tree in her path. She slammed the brakes, felt her car slide, then fishtail. She spun her wheel and tapped her accelerator to pull her out of the slide.

Her engine roared and her lungs constricted as

the car scrambled for purchase on the slick surface. She heard the ping of gravel hitting her paint. Gravel was better than slick asphalt, she decided. She'd be out of this mess in a minute. Then she'd stop, restart her heart and go home and cuddle Clem.

She might even pull those blankets up around her head, just for a little while.

But those thoughts were short-lived when she felt the car bounce over some uneven ground right before she felt the nose of the car dipping. Her vehicle slid down an embankment, its underside scraping over rocks and debris, and she looked out her window onto a gully containing swiftly running, black water. Her veins iced up and panic closed her throat. She was heading for that cold, foul water. God, there had to be something she could do to save herself, but her brain refused to engage.

Clem's beautiful face, those bright blue eyes and impish smile, swam across her vision as water covered her feet and soaked her jeans. As it crawled up her thighs, she felt Clem's arms around her neck, her gentle breath on her face.

Open the damn window, woman.

The voice in her head was from the past, but his tone was hard and demanding. Vivi slapped her hand on the button and the window slid down. A hard wave of water rocked her sideways, but she felt a strong hand on her shoulder and a comforting presence.

You can do this. Just keep calm.

Why was she hearing Camden McNeal's voice in

her head? She looked to the passenger seat, almost expecting to see the sexy ex–oil rigger there, tall and broad and so damn sexy. Clem's eyes in a masculine, tough face.

Take a deep breath...and another...

The water hit her chin and drops of dirt smacked her lips. Vivi took in another deep breath as water covered her head.

Hold on to the wheel and release your seat belt...

She pushed the lever and felt the seat belt drift away. Without it anchoring her to her seat, she felt buffeted by the water. Panic clawed at her stomach, twisting her brain. A twig scraped over her eyebrow and Vivi closed her eyes. What was the point of keeping them open? She couldn't see a damn thing as it was.

Survival instinct kicked in and she banged the frame of the open window, fighting the urge to haul in a breath.

She had to live. She had a little girl to raise. Grabbing the frame, she fought the water, scrabbling as she placed her feet against the console and tried to push herself through the open window. But she felt like she was trying to push through a concrete wall.

Wait five seconds and try again...

I don't have five damn seconds, Vivi mentally screamed.

Sure you do.

Vivi cursed him, her hands gripping the door frame. Five thousand one, five thousand two—God, she needed air—five thousand—

She couldn't wait any longer. Completely convinced that she was about to die, Vivi pushed against the console, pulled against the window frame and shot out of the car. It was dark and cold and scary, but there was light above her. She'd head for that. Light was good, light was safety...

Light meant Clem.

She was so close—her fingers were an inch from the surface—but her lungs were about to burst. Another kick, another pull...

Vivi's head broke the surface and she pulled in one life-affirming breath before darkness hauled her away.

Camden McNeal placed his palm on the window of his home office and looked out at the disappearing fog. He rolled his shoulders, trying to ease the tension in his shoulders and his back. He'd swallowed some painkillers a half hour ago, but the vise squeezing his brain had yet to release its claws. He felt like he was about to jump out of his skin.

Lifting his coffee mug to his lips, he took a large sip, enjoying the smooth taste of the expensive imported roast. He waited for the warmth to hit his stomach, but when it did, it burned rather than comforted. What the hell was wrong with him?

Yeah, the past few days hadn't been fun. Houston had been slapped senseless by a devastating storm and there were many people out there who were in dire straits, although he wasn't one of them. Not this time.

Count your blessings, McNeal...

Punching a number on his phone, he waited impatiently for Ryder to answer his call. "Cam, everything okay with you?"

His old boss and mentor had a way of making Cam feel steadier. Ryder was rock solid, as a colleague and a friend, and it never hurt to have someone like him standing in your corner. "My office is still under water and mud. All my computers are fried."

"Nasty. Hope you backed up," Ryder said.

All the time. "Yep, to a cloud server, so no information has been lost. But two of my guys have lost their houses and possessions." He already had plans in place to get them back on their feet.

"I've closed the office and told my people to care for their homes and families," Cam added.

"Yeah, I think that's standard procedure at the moment. Money and business can wait. There's more important work to do," Ryder agreed. "I spent yesterday working at a shelter. Did you go out last night?"

"Yeah, I was in one of the worst affected areas of the city—and one of the poorest. It was a community search effort to find some missing children. Two of them were found, but the third, a teenage boy, is still missing," Cam told Ryder.

Was that why he was so tense, so worried? He knew what it was like to feel abandoned, to be scared. Sure, he'd never been swept away in a flood, but he did have an idea how it felt to be poor, to live within a world that didn't seem to give a damn about people at the bottom of the pile.

He understood what it felt like to have poverty as your constant companion and hope an emotion you no longer believed in.

Cam's thoughts were pulled up short when Ryder spoke.

"Did you hear that a body was found at the construction site?"

Cam pushed his shoulders back, intrigued by Ryder's statement. "Are you talking about the TCC construction site? Sterling Perry's land?"

"Yes."

The establishment of a Houston branch of the Texas Cattleman's Club and control of it was Ryder and Sterling Perry's latest battle in a decades-old war. Both Stirling and Ryder believed that they were best suited to be the inaugural president of the new club, both wanted to be the first to create the vision of the first TCC in Houston. Neither suffered from a lack of self-confidence.

Cam knew that he'd be one of the first to be invited to join the exclusive club and the opportunity to do business with the other members, both in Houston and in Royal would be worth putting up with the politics and drama. And there seemed to be a lot of drama.

"What caused the accident?" Cam asked.

"A couple of bullets to the chest and a crushed skull."

So, not an accident then.

After discussing the murder and more TCC business, Cam disconnected the call. Walking away from the window and the view of his foggy gardens, he slumped into his butter-soft leather office chair. He tipped his head back and closed his eyes, the photograph of the missing kid flashing on the big screen behind his eyes. Dark hair, dark eyes, a sullen smile. Yeah, he recognized the look of despair in Rick Gaines's eyes, the belief that life was constantly looking for a way to slap him sideways.

It was possible that within a year or two, without help or intervention, Rick would be breaking into cars, dealing, or perhaps even be in a gang. He'd be another lost boy, flirting with jail or addiction. Cam recognized him instantly. After all, wasn't that exactly who he'd been?

Lost, lonely, confused. And Cam couldn't help wondering if Rick was even missing. Nobody had seen him fall into the water; he was simply unaccounted for. There was always the possibility that he'd used the flood as an opportunity to run away from his crappy life. Cam understood. When you were struggling to survive, you used the breaks you received…

Your childhood is behind you. That isn't your life anymore. You are now, and have been for a while, the master of your own destiny.

Cam swallowed the rest of his coffee, annoyed with himself. He didn't have time to wallow around in the cesspool of his past. He still had a massive company to run. Pulling his keyboard toward him, Cam opened his email program and grimaced at the flood of messages. Yep, as he'd expected, the financial world hadn't stopped turning. A couple of clients of his venture capital firm expressed their sympathy about the situation in Houston, but most didn't bother. It didn't affect them, so why waste the energy?

Cam was midway through typing a response to a Singaporean client when his ringing phone broke his concentration. He glanced at the display, didn't recognize the number and considered ignoring the call. Then he remembered that he'd asked the search coordinator to inform him if they located Rick. This could be an update, so he needed to take the call. He hit the speaker button with an impatient finger. "McNeal."

"Camden McNeal?"

"That's me."

"Excellent. You have been listed as the emergency contact number of a Vivianne Donner. I regret to inform you that Ms. Donner was admitted into the ER this morning after a car accident. When can we expect you?"

Cam pushed a hand through his hair, confused. "I think you have the wrong person. I don't know anyone by that name."

"I have your cell number, sir. You are Camden McNeal, owner of McNeal, Inc., and you live in River Oaks?"

"Yeah, that's correct—"

"You might not know her, but she sure knows you. So, my question remains, how soon can we expect you?"

* * *

Cam paced into the lobby of the hospital, his long stride eating up the distance between the doors and the nurses station. He dodged a nurse pushing a pregnant woman in a wheelchair and noticed that the dad-to-be was on the verge of panic. *Rather him than me*, Cam thought. He was the product of two of the most dysfunctional people in the world and what he knew about parenting would fit on a pinhead.

His father had taught him how to steal, to hustle, to slip and slide through life, but mostly his parents had taught him that he could only ever rely on, and take care of, himself. He didn't think he had it in him to put someone else's needs and wants above his own. It wasn't something he'd been shown how to do.

And the one time he'd tried, the only time he'd laid his heart at someone's feet, ring in his hand, Emma had stomped all over it with her three-inch stilettos, her expression a mixture of genuine disbelief and pity.

Darling, you're great in bed, but you're not exactly someone to take into a ballroom. Or into a boardroom, or home to Daddy. You're someone to screw, to keep in the shadows. Marry you? You're ambitious, Cam, I'll give you that, but I'm out of your league.

It had been ten years ago, but, despite her recently making it clear that she'd made a mistake by walking out on him, her little speech was imprinted on his brain, possibly because it closely resembled his father's words of non-encouragement. *"You're a Mc-*

*Neal, you'll never amount to much. None of us ever
have and you won't be the first."*

His bank statement and long lists of assets refuted
that statement. But Cam was a realist: he might be
good at business, but he'd make a lousy father and
husband. Hell, judging by how fast that nameless girl
in Tarrin left his bed three years ago, he wasn't even
that great at one-night stands. Sex, he was good at that,
but not so much at the touchy feely stuff woman liked.

Cam slapped his hands on the counter and met the
weary eyes of the nurse behind it. "I got a call about
a woman who put my name down as an emergency
contact. I'm Camden McNeal."

"Patient name?"

Cam tried to recall his earlier conversation. "Dun-
bar? Dun…something?"

"Donner? Vivianne Donner?"

Cam shrugged. The name didn't mean any more
to him now than it had earlier. The nurse tapped her
keyboard and nodded. "Room 302. She has severe
concussion and she needs a ride home, and someone
to take care of her when she gets there. Down the
hall, turn right and she'll be on your left."

Cam looked at the long hallway and sighed. Well,
it looked like he was about to meet Ms. Donner and
maybe he'd find out why he was listed as her emergency contact. Come to think of it, who was listed
as *his* emergency contact? Had he ever listed anyone? Not that he could recall.

Reaching the closed door to room 302, Cam

knocked gently. And when he received no reply, he
eased open the door. He glanced toward the bed and
waited for his eyes to adjust to the dim light.

His first impressions were of a long, slim body
topped by a cloud of curls the color of lightly toasted
caramel. His stomach rumbled at the thought of food.
He couldn't remember when he'd last eaten, as it had
been a busy, physically draining twenty-four hours.
He needed to talk to the woman, get her to take his
name off her papers and get some food. Maybe then
his headache would finally start to dissipate.

Cam flipped on the overhead light and it took a
minute, maybe more, to realize that his eyes weren't
playing tricks on him, that his imagination wasn't
running riot. He rested his hands on the bed next to
her thigh and ordered his racing heart to slow down,
his lungs to pull in air. He closed his eyes, re-centered
himself and then forced them open again.

Yep, she was still there.

Cam stared down at that stunning face, his heart
pounding against his chest in a fight-or-flight reaction. It had been three years, give or take, since he'd
seen her last, and damn, she looked, well, *amazing*.
Sure, she had three stitches holding a cut together
on a finely arched eyebrow, a bruise on her cheek
and a scrape across her jaw, and a deep cut on her
bottom lip, but her injuries didn't take away from
her drop-him-to-his-knees beauty. She'd lost weight
and looked like a puff of wind would blow her away.

Turning, Cam saw the chair next to the bed. He

hooked his foot around its legs and dragged it toward him. He dropped down into it and placed his forearms on his thighs, resisting the urge to shake her awake. What the hell game was she playing? She had to be playing one, because, let's be honest, everyone did.

He wasn't sure if she'd played him then, but he was certain she was playing him now. Cam stared at her as memories of that dive bar rolled over him. It had been a crap hole, little more than a shack serving watered-down drinks to the ranch hands and the refinery crews working in the area.

He'd been aware of her—Vivianne, he now had a name to go with the stunning face—the moment she stepped into the dive bar, as had every other man in the place. She'd looked so damn young and so very vulnerable with the shot glass in her hand, her eyes on the fiery liquid. He expected her to push it away, to turn tail and run, but she'd squared her shoulders and tossed the liquor back, blinking furiously as she swallowed. She'd banged her glass down, ordered another and slowly, oh so slowly, turned those brown-black eyes in his direction.

"One down, two more experiments to go."

He'd lifted his beer bottle in her direction, noting her long legs in tight, faded denim and the way her white T-shirt hugged the curves of her breasts and skimmed a board-flat stomach.

She was older than he initially thought, somewhere in her midtwenties, yet while they might be close in age, he'd figured he'd lived a thousand more lifetimes—all of them harder and rougher than hers.

He should've ignored her, finished his beer and left, but he'd turned to face her and cocked his head. "You a scientist, sweetheart?"

She'd ignored him at first, taken the second shot and tossed it down her throat. He'd never managed to forget her answer. She'd wrinkled her nose as she decided how to answer. "Nope. Tonight I'm going to see what being normal feels like."

"There are better bars in better places," Cam had told her, hoping that she'd walk out and leave him to his beer and his loneliness. He knew how to handle his liquor and his solitude, but she had him wanting to drink less and talk more.

She'd plopped that spectacular butt down on the seat next to him, her knee brushing against the outside of his thigh. He'd felt a bolt of desire skitter up his thigh and lodge in his balls. He'd swelled and groaned. He wasn't a kid, so why was he getting turned on by a light touch and a woman who looked like the girl next door and smelled like wildflowers?

"But I can't get to those places and you look like fun."

Cam had almost smiled at that. Him fun? She couldn't be more wrong. He'd thought about leaving her there in the bar, about going back to his motel room with a six-pack, but he couldn't leave her there alone. So he'd bought her a beer and then they'd moved on to a diner for burgers and ended the evening with fantastic sex in a motel room. No names, no expectations and, yeah, he'd had fun.

He'd liked her.

And now, after three years, she was back in his life, lying in a hospital room, dressed in a hospital gown, banged up and bruised. With his name as her emergency contact number. And like back then, his mouth was dry, his heart was thumping and his pants were tight against his crotch. *Peachy.*

What the hell was going on here?

Cam felt her leg jerk and his eyes shot to her face. Her eyelids flickered, and he waited for that burst of brown, braced himself for the sexual punch that was sure to follow. She groaned, half lifted her hand and then dropped it to the bed, as if the action required more energy than she was capable of. Those long eyelashes lifted and he watched as she took a moment to focus. Her mouth tilted at the corners and her expression softened.

"Camden?"

So she knew him, recognized him. Cam frowned when her eyes drifted closed again. Oh, no, he wasn't going to sit next to her bed like a lovelorn admirer waiting for her to wake up. He was exhausted and hungry, dammit. Cam tapped her hand with his finger and slowly her eyelids lifted.

The tip of a pink tongue darted across her top lip and Cam ignored the bolt of lust as he remembered that tongue on his abs, going lower. She'd been inexperienced in that department but very enthusiastic…

Down, boy.

He rubbed his hand over his face, and when he dropped his hand again, the confusion in her eyes was replaced by panic. "Where am I? Where's Clem? Is she okay?"

She started to push herself up, groaning as she sat up. She pushed the covers away and swung those sexy, bare legs to the side. Cam immediately realized that she was trying to climb out of bed. He shot up and placed a hand on her shoulder, pinning her to the pillow. She slapped his hand away and went for the IV, trying to pull the needle from her arm.

"I've got to get to Clem. Let me go, dammit!" Her breath hitched and panic made her words run together. "What's the time? How late is it? Where's my phone?"

Cam looked at his watch. "It's shortly past eleven."

"It's still Friday morning?"

At his nod, her shoulders dropped three inches and the cords in her neck loosened. She slumped back against her pillow and closed her eyes. "Thank God." She gripped the sheet and twisted the fabric between her fingers. When she spoke again, her voice was thin with pain and exhaustion. "I need to make a call. Can I borrow your phone?"

"Not until I get some answers," Cam told her, stepping back and folding his arms against his chest.

Vivianne released a frustrated sigh. In her eyes he saw a solid streak of stubborn under the obvious exhaustion. "I understand that. But you're not going to get another word out of me until I make a call."

It wasn't worth arguing about. Reaching into the back pocket of his jeans, he pulled out his phone, tapped in the code and handed it to her.

She shook her head. "Sorry, the world is still a bit fuzzy. Can you dial for me?"

Cam punched in the number she gave him, and when it started to ring, he handed the phone over. Vivianne placed her fingers on her forehead before speaking. "Charlie? Is Clem okay?"

Evidently the response reassured her. Those sexy shoulders dropped and the hand gripping the sheet relaxed. Cam tipped his head to the side, thinking that watching her was like witnessing a balloon losing its air. Suddenly she looked paler, more fragile, ten times smaller. And a hundred times more vulnerable.

He stepped forward, realized he was about to pull her into his arms, to offer what comfort he could, and immediately stepped back. What the hell? He didn't do comfort; he wasn't the type.

Vivianne gnawed at her bottom lip, wincing when she encountered the cut she'd made earlier. "Thanks, Charlie. I'll see you later this afternoon, maybe a little earlier if I can."

As if. According to the nurse, she had a concussion and that normally meant an overnight stay. He'd be happy to watch her all night. But only because he wanted to know what she was up to. Not because she was freakin' gorgeous. And not because he found her fascinating, or because he couldn't imagine walking out of this room without knowing when he was going to see her again.

He was just tired. And hungry. That was why he was acting so out of character. *Had to be.*

"Thanks, Charlie."

Cam jammed his hands into the front pockets of his jeans and glowered at her. "Ready to start talking?"

Vivianne sighed. "I don't suppose I have much of a choice."

"Not really, no."

"I'm Vivi Donner, by the way."

Vivi suited her better than *Vivianne*. He rolled the name around his mind and could easily imagine himself whispering it as he kissed her, painting it on her skin as he tongued her. Sighing it as he slid into her hot, wet warmth. Cam gave himself a mental punch to the temple.

Yeah, he was still attracted to her but so what? He was frequently attracted to women. He was a guy and that was what guys did. It was simple biology. It didn't *mean* anything.

"Let's start off with you telling me how you ended up in a hospital with stitches and scrapes and more bruises than an MMA fighter."

Vivi pushed back that heavy hair and he caught a whiff of citrus and dank water. "According to the nurse, who spoke to the responding EMT, I was driving and it was really foggy. I slid off the road into a gully filled with fast-moving water. I remember going into the water and nothing much after that. The next time I came around, I was in this bed."

Every cell in his body iced over. Few people knew how to escape a car filled with water, yet she had. Thank God.

"A policeman saw me go off the road. The working theory is that I pushed myself out the window and swam to the surface. The cop saw me come up, but then I was hit by a branch and swept away. Luckily a rescue boat was downstream from me and they hauled me out. I don't remember anything after my car hit the water."

God, she'd been fantastically, ridiculously lucky. She obviously had a dozen angels sitting on her shoulder.

He desperately wanted to find out why she'd run out on him that night, why she'd insinuated herself back into his life now. She'd known him as a greasy rigger, solidly blue collar. He'd been good for a night, a roll in the sheets, and he hadn't really been surprised when he'd turned over and she wasn't there.

He was a ship in the night, here today and gone tomorrow, He only ever indulged in fun that lasted a few hours, max. He was not a guy someone like her— classy and warm—wanted to face over coffee in the morning.

Was she back only because his bank accounts were fat and his social standing solid? Because he was now apparently acceptable?

Cam felt the sharp burn beneath his rib cage

and cursed. He cursed himself for caring what she thought and he cursed her for dropping back into his comfortable, and predictable, life. He'd never forgotten her and he hated her for that. He didn't like connections, ties, memories.

Cam walked over to the window and stared out into the hospital parking lot. There, close to the entrance, was his luxury SUV, top of the line, ridiculously expensive. He lived in a big-ass house, had numerous, hefty bank accounts. He had, he reluctantly admitted, everything he'd ever wanted, yet this brown-eyed woman made him feel like his world was shifting, that something was changing.

Vivi's reappearance in his life was going to rock him to the soles of his feet.

Cam sighed before turning around. "Why am I your emergency contact person, Vivianne?"

This time Vivi gripped the sheets with both hands, and whatever color was left in her face drained away. She stared at him, licking her lips, and he could see the turmoil in those eyes, the trembling of her bottom lip. "I have a daughter, Clementine. I call her Clem. She's two years old and you are her father."

Two

Telling a guy he had a child was a hell of a way to clear a room.

Vivi looked at the door Camden had slammed closed, half expecting him to reappear and start yelling. When twenty seconds passed, then thirty, then a minute, she finally released the breath she was holding. While she was better at confrontation now than she'd been years ago, she still didn't like to argue. The same, so she'd heard, couldn't be said for Camden Mc-Neal. All her research—and she'd researched him to death—pointed to the fact that Cam McNeal, oil rigger turned venture capitalist, treated business like a boxing ring and went in swinging. He was tough, demanding and controlling, and he didn't take any prisoners, ever.

Neither, it was reported, did he suffer fools. The business press called him a blizzard, cool and deadly, but Vivi thought they'd mischaracterized him. He wasn't cold. Beneath that icy facade resided a passionate man. A man fully in control of his volatile emotions. But cold and unfeeling? Oh, hell, no.

Vivi pulled her knees up and groaned as every muscle in her body protested. She was exhausted both mentally and physically, but she was sure there was no chance of sleep anytime soon, since she knew she hadn't seen the last of Cam this morning. Instinctively she understood that Cam had only left the room so that she wouldn't witness his anger, disappointment or shock. Or all three. He obviously needed some time to regain his famous control. That was okay; she needed to regain hers, too.

Three years and he was still earth-shatteringly sexy.

Vivi heard the ding of an incoming message and looked at Cam's smartphone, which she still held in her hand. Swiping her thumb across the screen, she saw the dial pad and impulsively dialed Joe's number, needing to connect with the only person she considered family.

After a brief explanation to Joe about the accident, Vivi told him that she was fine and that he didn't need to rush across town.

"But how are you going to get home? Pick up Clem?" Joe demanded.

"I have someone here," Vivi admitted. When she'd made Camden Clem's guardian and her emergency contact she'd never considered that he might actually need to be called. "Camden McNeal."

Joe waited a beat before snapping out his question. "And why is Cam McNeal with you, Vivianne?"

Here came the hard part.

He'd been the first man she'd noticed on entering that hole-in-the-wall bar three blocks down from her mom's house in Tarrin, a small town west of Houston. He was lounging on a bar stool, watching her with bright blue eyes. His light brown hair had been longer then, touching the collar, though now it was expensively cut. His tall, muscular body seemed harder now, as was his attitude.

"So, I've told you a little of my history with my parents," she began.

"A little, mostly that you were fed a steady diet of anti-government and end-of-the-world BS from your father and you're-going-to-fry-if-you-don't-listen propaganda from your mother," Joe said, always impatient with intolerance.

"I was an only child with ridiculously overprotective parents, so college was out of the question. Dating—unless it was arranged through my mother—was frowned upon, and socializing outside of their tight social circle was not acceptable. Drinking and dancing and sex? Hell, no."

"And hell, as you were frequently told, was where you'd end up if you flirted with those vices."

"I told you that my dad died and that the family money was placed into a trust, controlled by lawyers who were my dad's friends, and every decision we made had to go through the lawyers. I was so angry."

"I'm still not seeing the connection to Camden McNeal."

"After leaving the lawyers and my mother after the funeral, I ended up in a bar, and later, in Cam McNeal's bed. And with his baby in my belly.

"My mother was angry with me for embarrassing her on the day they buried my father, but she was incandescently furious when I told her I was pregnant. Basically, she disowned me," Vivi explained.

"Can I track her down and give her a piece of my mind?"

Vivi smiled at Joe's outrage. God, she loved this man.

"You must've been so scared, Viv."

"I was, but I also felt empowered. And free."

She'd faced a tough, uncertain future, but it was *her* future, one she'd created. "I thought about contacting Clem's father but I didn't know his surname and had no idea where he worked."

But more than that, she hadn't wanted to put herself under anyone's control again. This was her life and she was responsible for herself and her baby. She'd made this bed and she was determined to show herself that she could sleep in it.

"I relied on public assistance and bounced from job to job, first juggling pregnancy and then a tiny baby as I tried to earn enough to support us both. Then I found work with you."

Those first few months after Clem's birth had been super tough, but life had improved when she found steady work as a dishwasher at The Rollin' Smoke. She'd met Charlie, the widowed mother of one of the servers, who ran a childcare service from home. Finally, after placing Clem with someone who was both affordable and loving, her confidence had grown. She'd pestered Joe to both teach and promote her, and the result was that she'd risen through the ranks at a record pace. Line chef in three months, sous chef in six, head chef within the next year.

"And sometime, I'm guessing recently, you bumped into Cam again. Probably at the restaurant, since Ryder Currin introduced him to my place."

Nail on head. "Three months ago, I was off duty but I went into Rollin' with Clem at lunchtime to check on my kitchen. You grabbed Clem and took her into the restaurant to meet the customers."

"She is the grandchild of my heart."

Vivi felt the hard ball of emotion clog her throat. "I looked through the kitchen window and saw two men sitting at the coveted VIP table." And just like earlier, she'd found her head swimming and her throat constricting. She'd looked into that hard, sexy face and realized that her baby's dad was eating at her restaurant.

"I asked Gemma who he was."

She still remembered the words from the waitress. "The younger hottie is Camden McNeal, venture capitalist. He's one of those guys who went from rags to fabulous riches in a heartbeat." Gemma had added, grinning, "So sexy."

He was. And his sexiness was the reason for the little girl she loved more than life itself.

"Since then I've wrestled with whether to contact McNeal, whether he had the right to know that he had a daughter," she told Joe. "One day I'd decide it was the right thing to do, and the next I was convinced that it was better to leave him in the dark."

They'd met when they were both poor, both in different places in their lives. They'd moved on from the people they were then, thank goodness, and while she was proud of her achievements, his rise to success had been stratospheric. According to her research— Google, mostly—he routinely refused personal interviews; it was reported that he was cynical, controlling and suspicious, not one for making friends easily.

"I kept thinking that if I showed up on his doorstep with Clementine, he'd accuse me of being a gold digger trying to cash in on his wealth. Or he'd want to take control of the situation. And of Clementine."

"Well, that's a moot point now, isn't it?" Joe said, as blunt as always.

Maybe, but neither option was remotely acceptable. She didn't want his money. Nothing was more important to her than making it on her own, and she certainly wouldn't give Camden McNeal any say over her or her daughter's life. She'd lived under her parents' control, and she wasn't ever going back to that.

And then there was the little problem of her still being utterly, completely, ridiculously attracted to him. As much, or more, than she was three years ago. She just needed to see a photo of him online and her lungs constricted and heat rushed between her legs.

Not something she wanted to think about when she was having a conversation with the person who'd stepped into her father's shoes.

"But at the end of the day, Camden is, apart from my mother, Clem's only biological relative. I was so worried that, if something happened to me, Margaret would petition the courts for custody of Clem."

"I'd would've fought her," Joe assured her.

He would and she loved him for it. "But, because you are close to seventy, Joe, and my mom is only in her early fifties, and a woman, she would've won. Even if I gave Clem to you, and I wanted to do that, I was told it would be easily challenged given your age and the fact that we're not related. On legal advice, I updated my will to give Cam custody and put him as my emergency contact number in case something bad happened."

And it so very nearly had.

And now, Camden McNeal, that gorgeous, billionaire badass, was back in her life.

He was the one thing he'd never thought he'd be.

In the hallway outside Vivi's room, Cam lifted his hand and saw his shakes. As a young kid, six or seven years old, when his dad left him alone, for days on end, his hand had never shaken. When he'd scaled buildings and crept past sleeping couples to steal wallets and jewelry, he'd shrugged off the nerves and kept his cool. The day he was arrested and heard that his father wouldn't bail him out, his hands hadn't trembled.

He was a dad, he had a kid…

Life had finally found the one thing, the only thing, that terrified him. Cam rested his head on the wall and fought the urge to slide down its smooth surface. Slapping his palms on the cool surface, he locked his knees and pulled in rhythmic breaths, desperately looking for control, for a measure of calm.

He had no idea how to be a father, a parent responsible for someone else. His father had only occasionally remembered to feed and clothe him. He'd taught him how to roll a cigarette, to spot a mark, to lift a wallet. He'd taught him to fight dirty, to run from cops and social workers, to distrust the system. He'd been more like a delinquent older brother than a father, and consequently all Cam knew about fatherhood was how *not* to be one. Had Vivi recognized that in him? Was that why she never informed him of his daughter? Clementine. Clem.

He had a daughter. Cam blinked furiously, annoyed at his moist eyes. Okay, she was only two, but he was no longer completely alone. There was another person in the world he was linked to. She was young and defenseless, but that link existed, it meant *something*.

Cam rubbed his hands over his face and pushed his fingers through his hair. What now? He couldn't prop up this wall for the rest of the day. At some point he'd have to go in and face Vivi, deal with the situation he found himself in. Cam glanced at Vivi's closed door and sighed. He also needed to deal with his instant, hot-as-hell attraction that was arcing between him and the mother of his child. *Supposed* mother of her child. Cam grabbed on to that cynical thought and held on with every fiber of his being. He just had her word that he was her kid's dad. She could be scamming him, running a con. If he was sensible, he'd walk out of here right now and demand a paternity test. He should wait for scientific proof…

No, that wasn't going to happen. He was upset, confused, utterly side-slapped by this news, but his gut instinct told him that she was telling the truth. He was a daddy.

God.

Cam watched a doctor and nurse walk toward him. They stopped at Vivi's door and handed him a harried greeting. They entered her room and he followed them in, standing at the back of the room out of their way as they approached the bed. Over their heads he saw her resigned expression.

"I'm fine," Vivi firmly stated, but Cam heard the tremor in her voice. "I need sleep and a couple of painkillers and I'll be fine."

"I went to med school and studied for a dozen years. Do you not think I should make that call?" the female doctor replied, amused. She jerked her head in his direction. "Someone you know?"

Vivi's eyes collided with his and Cam felt the air leave his lungs. God, she was so damn beautiful. He'd thought so three years ago but there was a strength to her now, a maturity that had been missing in that girl he'd slept with so long ago. Back then she'd been a fun night, a diversion, a break from a hard job and constant loneliness. Lying in that hospital bed, she was now…what? He didn't know.

"I know him," Vivi said, resigned. "When can I get discharged?"

The doctor examined her eyes as the nurse wound a blood pressure cuff around her arm. The doctor pushed and prodded Vivi's slim body before stepping back and folding her arms. "I will only discharge you if you promise not to drive."

Frustration flashed in Vivi's eyes. "My car is, I presume, waterlogged and at the bottom of a gully, so I won't be driving anywhere. I'll catch a cab or Uber."

The thought of her being trapped in that car iced his veins and Cam placed his palm on the wall to anchor him. He couldn't imagine a world, didn't want to imagine a world, that didn't have Vivi Donner in it. A surprising thought, given that he'd never expected to see her again.

Vivi released a small moan and Cam's eyes flew back to her distressed face. He quickly moved to her side, placing his hand on her thigh. "What is it? What's wrong?"

"No car, no money, no phone." Vivi bit her bottom lip and he saw fine dots of blood appear there because she'd reopened her cut.

"Stop biting your lip." Her eyes flashed at his order and he noticed irritation replacing fear. Good, he could work with anger; he'd couldn't cope with tears. "I have a car and money. I'll get you home." He ignored Vivi's annoyed squawk and looked at the doctor. "Since she has a concussion, must I wake her up every couple of hours?"

The doctor shook her head. "Not necessary. I'd suggest rest and lots of it." She directed a stern glance at Vivi. "You had a nasty experience, Miss Donner, but I also suspect that you've been burning the candle at both ends lately."

Vivi wouldn't meet her eyes, so Cam asked for an explanation.

"Ms. Donner is a bit thinner than I'd like, and those blue stripes under her eyes aren't the result of the accident but nights without sleep. She's also slightly anemic."

Vivi looked like she wanted to roll her eyes. "I am the single mother of an energetic toddler who isn't fond of sleep."

And just like that, both the nurse and doctor turned sympathetic. The nurse rested a hand on Vivi's shoulder and sighed. "Oh, honey." Without doubt, she was a mother, too, Cam thought.

The doctor shook her head. "I have a three-year-old and a six-year-old and a husband, and all three exhaust me. I feel your pain."

Cam thought they were laying it a little thick. How difficult could a two-year-old be? But Cam was bright enough to realize that if he disagreed, he might be verbally skewered by three mothers. Better to keep quiet. Safer, too.

"The point is," he said, pulling them back to the matter at hand, "I will take Vivi home."

Vivi looked mutinous. "That's not going to work for me."

"Well, it's the only way you're going to get discharged," the doctor told her. "No driving for twenty-four hours, plenty of rest and no physical activity."

Cam's eyes met Vivi's; her eyes widened and her cheeks turned a pretty pink. Sure, his thoughts kept wandering to the sex they'd shared, but because she'd suffered a smack to her head, he hadn't figured hers had, too. But that blush, spreading down her neck and disappearing under her hospital gown, told him a completely different story. Well, good.

No! *Hell*. They didn't need the complication of still being ridiculously attracted to each other. And acting on that attraction, which he really wanted to do, would just be stupid.

He'd made a point of not acting stupid, but damn, this time it was hard.

He saw confusion in her eyes, noticed her embarrassment. Cam hauled in a breath, saw that they were alone—when had the medical staff left?—and sat down on the edge of her bed. Unable to resist touching her, he allowed the tips of his fingers to trace the fine line of her jaw. "Hell of a day, huh?"

Vivi nodded. She started to pull her bottom lip between her teeth, but he tapped her lip and she let go. "You've really got to stop doing that."

"I know."

"I've got a better idea." He shouldn't be doing this, but he needed just one taste, one kiss. He needed to know whether she tasted as good as he remembered, or whether his imagination had played tricks on him for the past three years. One kiss couldn't hurt...

Could it?

Under his lips, hers were soft and silky. Holding her jaw, Cam moved his lips across hers, breathing in her scent, sweet flowers touched by dark waters. Keeping his kiss gentle because of the cut on her lip, he inhaled her breath and tasted her essence. He remembered her as being hot and sexy, but this woman, this new version of the girl he'd met, held more depth, was a hundred times more interesting. Her lips parted, and his tongue slid past her teeth and he tasted sweetness and sin, vulnerability and strength. Determination and independence masking a ribbon of fear.

Fear? What was she scared of?

He pulled back, looked into her eyes and saw that same emotion reflected in her eyes. A second later it was gone, shut up and put away. Vivi Donner was almost as good at masking her emotions as he was. The realization both intrigued and fascinated him, and the fact that he was both intrigued and fascinated worried him.

Complications weren't his thing.

Vivi swallowed and looked toward the door. "So, I guess if I want to get out of here, you're my ride."

Okay, she was ignoring the kiss, their crazy attraction. Maybe he should do the same. Yet his heart thumped when she picked up his wrist so that she could look at his watch. "If I can get home, I'd be able to sleep for a few hours before I need to collect Clem. Do you want to meet her?"

His heart bounced off his chest. He'd just found Vivi again and didn't know if he was up to meeting his daughter today. He hadn't had time to process any of this, and didn't think he even could.

"It was just a suggestion, Cam. You don't have to meet her if you don't want to. I'm not asking anything from you…not your time or money or input. So, really, no hard feelings if you say no."

Except that she would think that he was a wuss, that he wasn't man enough to acknowledge his child. If he walked away and ignored the situation, Vivi would think he was weak and selfish and a bit of a man-child. And she'd be right.

Suck it up, McNeal. She's had a near-death experience, escaped from a sinking car, got smacked around by river detritus and ended up in a hospital. If she can cope with all that, you can meet a two-year-old.

An ordinary two-year-old, maybe. His daughter? He wasn't so sure.

Vivi tipped her head to the side. "Getting a bit too real, huh?"

He thought about laughing her statement away— he could be charming when he chose to be—but decided to tell the truth. "Too real. Utterly surreal."

She twisted her lips and then her hands. "I suppose you want an explanation."

"Do you not think I deserve one?"

Vivi lifted one shoulder, as if silently admitting that she had her doubts. Dammit, what did she want from him? He dealt in black-and-white; gray was his least favorite color in the world. Cam was about to demand that she start explaining, when he caught her touching the back of her head, trying hard to contain her wince. He skimmed his eyes over the bruises on her arms and stood up, gripping the edge of the sheet.

He looked at Vivi. "I just want to see what we're dealing with. May I?"

At her nod, he pulled down the sheet. Her gown ended midthigh and she had a scrape on her thigh, a bruised knee and another bruise on her shin. God, she looked like she'd been hit by a tank.

Instead of protesting his examination of her body, Vivi just put her head against the pillow and closed her eyes. "I fell pregnant, but I didn't know your name—"

She didn't need to do this now. She shouldn't *have* to do this now. Feeling suddenly protective of her, he realized her explanations could wait until she felt stronger. Or when she was, at the very least, pain free.

He bent down and surprised himself by placing his lips on her forehead. This crazy situation would still be there. "Not now, Viv. Let's get you home."

Vivi forced her eyes open. "I'd like to be home, clean and be cuddling with Clem."

Cam nodded. "Lie there and rest and let me see if I can make that happen."

He wanted to take her home to his place, not hers, a place where he knew he could protect her.

Cam rolled his shoulders, irritated with himself.

The worst was over, what more could happen to her? Why was he so reluctant to leave her alone?

Press Release.
For Immediate Release.
Body Discovered at Texas Cattleman's Club, Houston Construction Site.

Yesterday, at 7:40 a.m., members of the Houston Police Department and emergency medical responders responded to a report of a male victim found at the west Houston construction site of the Texas Cattleman's Club, about two miles west of Highway 10. Upon the arrival of first responders, the male was pronounced deceased at the scene.

At this time the identity of the male is unknown. According to the medical examiner, the cause of death is due to a gunshot wounds to the chest. Houston Police Department detectives are investigating with the assistance of the district attorney's office. Identification of the victim and an accurate time of death are still to come. A case of homicide has been opened and no further information is currently available.

If anyone has information regarding this incident they are asked to contact…

Glass-wall offices meant eyes were on me, so I skimmed over the media release. Nothing in my face or my demeanor reflected my inner turmoil or hinted at my racing heart. I looked at my fingers, pleased to see that they weren't shaking. I pushed the paper to one side. Reading media releases has been a long-standing habit and one I am grateful for.

Reading the morning papers is another habit I've cultivated, and I pulled the pile toward me, and skimmed their pages for more information. Speculation was rampant but there was not much more to be gleaned. It was the same information, padded and puffed, but nothing new and nothing to link me to the murder at the Texas Cattleman's Club building site.

Thank God.

Determined not to miss anything—the smallest bit of knowledge might be the difference between me meeting a needle while wearing prison orange or not—I skimmed the short article buried on page 3 of a local newspaper and frowned. Taking a breath, I read it again, slower this time.

The victim has not been identified and the time of death is unknown. Like so many other properties in the city, the construction site experienced extensive flooding thanks to the once-in-a-generation storm, making identification of the victim or forensics difficult.

That statement wasn't accurate. I thought back to that morning, remembering the sharp snap of the pistol firing, the blood on a white shirt, his wide, terrified eyes as I stood over him, his life draining away. For insurance, I stared into his eyes and pulled the trigger again, sending another bullet into his already mutilated chest cavity. Fighting my panic, I acted fast and removed his wallet, his distinctive watch, the bracelets on his thick wrist, anything that might make identifying him easier. Dropping the concrete slab on his face had been added insurance, because the more time I put between his death and his identification, the better. I never imagined that I would get a helping hand from Mother Nature. The recent flood was a blessing in disguise. For me, at least.

I hid my smile and power-read through the rest of the article. Nobody working on the Perry Construction crew is talking; one worker hinted at a company gag order being in place.

At my suggestion, Sterling Perry sent an email to the construction foreman, telling him in no uncertain terms that any worker caught talking to the press would be summarily dismissed, and it pleased me that his orders were being obeyed. Excellent, since I wasn't in the mood to follow up on the issue, mostly because my interest might raise suspicion and I needed to fly under the radar. Becoming a suspect would be intolerable and jail simply wouldn't suit me.

After folding the newspaper into a perfect rectangle, I placed it on top of the pile of other precisely folded papers and leaned back in my chair. So far, so good. Nobody suspected me, nobody ever will. Thank God, because I still have a score, or three or four, to settle with Sterling Perry and his family. And with his archenemy Ryder Currin...

In my case, the enemy of my enemy was not my friend...

Three

In the hospital parking lot, Cam opened the passenger door of his SUV and gestured Vivi inside. Vivi inhaled that new-car smell and looked at the expensive seats, the massive dashboard. This was a $300,000 car, and, because she couldn't leave the hospital in a flimsy gown, her filthy, still-wet sneakers were about to touch the spotless carpet, her mud-streaked jeans were going to make contact with his butter-soft leather seats.

Nope, she couldn't. She'd take a cab home.

"Problem?" Cam asked, his voice brushing her ear. Vivi felt the heat of his body behind her and saw his big hand grip the car frame above her head, his expensive watch glinting in the sunlight. He'd come a long way in three years. A beat-up truck to this beauty, work boots to $300 cowboy boots, functional denim to designer labels. She'd come a long way, too, and she was proud of herself, but man, Cam had her beat.

It wasn't a competition, Donner, and Cam didn't have a child to deal with. You've done okay, you know you have.

Clem was safe and happy and lacked for nothing. Sure, it would be nice to have a little more stashed away for a rainy day, to have a place of her own, but it could be worse. She could still be back at her mother's, going to her church, living a small life in a small community. *Count your blessings, dammit. You have everything you need...*

"Can I help you up?"

Vivi half turned and lifted her hands. "I can't get in there, Cam."

Cam frowned. "And why not?"

"This car is brand new. I am filthy. My clothes are still damp and muddy, and I reek of ditchwater."

Spreading his legs, Cam folded his arms across his chest, and Vivi appreciated the bulge of his biceps straining the band of his T-shirt. He shook his head. "Get in the car, Vivianne."

"I can't!"

Muttering a curse, Cam moved quickly. He gripped her waist, lifted her and easily deposited her into the soft leather chair. He placed a hand on her thigh and one on her shoulder and glared at her. "It's a *car.* I don't give a damn whether it gets dirty or not. Carpets can get cleaned, leather seats can get wiped down." He leaned forward and sniffed; amusement jumped into his eyes. "Though you could do with a shower."

Vivi blushed. "I know, I'm really sorry."

Cam's thumb found the rip on the knee of her jeans and caressed that small patch of bare skin. Vivi watched his eyes darken, and emotion she couldn't identify flashed in his eyes. "You nearly died, Vivi. I'd rather have you here, dirty and a little smelly, than dead and gone."

He was so direct, so damn to the point, and Vivi liked it. She liked the way he said what he meant, whether she wanted to hear it or not. Her parents had been so passive-aggressive, so manipulative that she'd spent most of her life trying to decipher what they meant, second-guessing her responses and re-actions, never quite sure if she was doing or saying the right thing. She liked direct people; she always knew where she stood with them.

"We done with this conversation?" Cam asked her.

Vivi sighed. "Yeah."

The corners of his mouth lifted. "'Bout time."

He slammed the car door shut and Vivi pulled the seat belt down as she watched him walk around the hood of the SUV to the driver's door. Long strides, messy hair, stubble on his strong jaw. He was such a man, an alpha male in his prime.

Cam pulled open his door, settled into his seat and reached for a pair of expensive sunglasses resting in the console. He half lifted them to his face when he stopped to look at her. He held out the sunglasses to her. "How's your head? Do you want to use these?"

Vivi was touched by his casual offer. Her head was pounding, and she couldn't look out of the windshield without feeling like the sun was piercing her eyes with thousand-degree needles. Her fingers brushed Cam's as she took the glasses from him and she felt another shiver of awareness. God, he was hot. And under that gruff, sweet.

"Thank you." Vivi placed the too-big sunglasses on her face and sighed with relief. The lenses cut the glare and her headache retreated from excruciating to simply horrible.

Heading toward the exit of the parking lot, Cam sent her a glance. "Where to?"

"Are you sure you don't mind driving me?" Vivi asked, half turning in her seat so that she could rest her pounding head on the soft seat. "It might be a bit out of your way."

"The address, Vivi."

Vivi recited her address and Cam activated the on-board GPS.

At the first red light, Cam turned his head to look at her. "You up to some conversation?"

"About Clem?"

"She's the most important part of what I want to talk about," Cam replied, accelerating across the intersection. He shifted, picked up speed and shifted again. He drove like he made love, with complete confidence and self-assurance. Was there anything about this man she didn't find sexy?

"I'm impatient by nature," he said, "but if you can't talk now, I will wait. Reluctantly."

Vivi pulled her eyes off his hands and sat up, stretching out her legs. She stifled a groan, her muscles screaming, volubly reminding her that she'd been in an accident, that she'd narrowly escaped drowning in a car.

Cam's hand tightened on the steering wheel. "Now that I know about Clem, what are you expecting from me? Child support is a given. Give me a number and I'll set up a recurring monthly payment."

Cam had gone from zero to sixty and she was trailing far, far behind. "But what about proof? Paternity test? Don't you want some sort of guarantee that she's yours?"

Cam's brief look was arrow sharp and laser intense. "Is she mine?"

"Yes."

"Okay, then. Let's move on."

Vivi stared at him, shocked. How could he just take what she was saying at face value? How could he trust her? She didn't trust anybody, especially when it came to Clem.

"Vivianne, thanks to my past, I've got a near infallible BS detector. I can spot a lie from fifty paces. If you want to go through the whole dog and pony show of paternity tests, we can do that, but it's not necessary. You say she's mine, I believe you. The end."

What kind of past gave a person the ability to read people, to spot lies? Vivi really wanted to know. She opened her mouth to ask, saw Cam's don't-go-there expression and backed off. Okay, message received.

Going back to his previous statement, she said, "I don't need anything from you."

She didn't. She and Clem were fine. She had a good job—the restaurant would reopen soon, any other option would not be tolerated!—and a great support system, and she was, finally, happy, dammit. She was the master of her destiny, the captain of her ship. She would not allow some rich guy, no matter how sexy and how much she wanted to kiss him, to walk into her life and rearrange it. She'd cried and fought and hustled and worked her butt off to be independent. She would never allow anyone to control her actions again.

Vivi placed her hand on her stomach and hauled in a deep breath. "We don't need you, Camden."

She heard his swift intake of breath and her eyes flew up to his. For a moment, for a split second, she suspected that she'd hurt him, that her words were like arrows hitting his soul. Then he turned those cool, mocking eyes on hers and sent her a cold smile. "Well, then, if that was the way you wanted to play it, then you shouldn't have put my name as your emergency contact." He gestured to her muddy clothing. "Because, you know, sometimes emergencies happen."

Crap. He had her there. Folding her arms across her chest, Vivi stared straight ahead, feeling like her head was about to split open. She'd made the choice to list Cam as her emergency contact, to give him custody of Clem in case of an unfortunate event.

What she'd never expected to happen actually had. And that meant dealing with Cam, working her way through this quagmire. As much as she wanted to, she simply couldn't wish him away. And even if she could, she doubted that she would. He was so compelling, utterly mesmerizing. His charisma hadn't dimmed, and he was, if possible, even more attractive than he'd been years ago. He was one of those men people paid attention to, possibly because he didn't give a damn whether you did or not.

He wasn't an easy man, nor was he comfortable, but, hell, he was interesting.

Cam reached down, flipped open the lid to the console between them and pulled out a bottle of aspirin. He tossed it into her lap and, reaching behind her seat, pulled a bottle of water from a pack on the floor. "Take a couple and then start talking."

It was one command she was prepared to obey. Five minutes later, after swallowing most of the bottle of water, she felt a little stronger. "What do you want to discuss?"

Cam's took a moment to reply. "That night…why did you leave?"

Because it was late, and she knew that her mom would be frantic. Because if she wasn't home by dawn, there was a strong possibility that her mom would call the church prayer line and every male member of the church would scour Tarrin for her. She'd known that she was in for a verbal thrashing for leaving the funeral and will reading, but if her mother found out she'd visited a bar and slept with a stranger… Well, hell, Satan would've taken cover.

But nothing compared to the meltdown her mom had descended into when she heard about her pregnancy. Hell, she was certain, was still in recovery mode.

"I didn't think that we had much more to say to one another. We drank, we danced, we slept together. We were done." Hooking up with Cam had been an act of defiance, of rebellion, and she'd never, not for one minute, thought that it could last beyond dawn. That was why they hadn't bothered with names, why they hadn't shared anything personal. They had been two people who were attracted to each other, using each other to alleviate their loneliness and have a brief physical connection. Had she read the evening wrong? Had he wanted more? Vivi frowned. "Did you want to see me again?"

Cam's jaw hardened, and he stared straight ahead. "It ended how it was expected to end."

Vivi couldn't help noticing that he didn't answer her question. She debated what to say next. She certainly wasn't going to tell him how her mother had reacted when she finally faced the fact that Vivi was pregnant, how she had screamed at Vivi for two days straight before tossing her out of the only home she'd ever known, into a strange and scary world.

Vivi tasted the same panic at the back of her throat

and reminded herself that she'd survived, then she'd flourished. She was okay, Clem was okay, life was good.

"I moved away from Tarrin and came to Houston."

"Why?"

Dammit, she didn't want to answer that question. She wondered how to respond without telling him too much and decided to keep it simple. "I wasn't welcome there anymore." She saw him open his mouth and began to speak again before he could lob another question her way. "I found a place to stay, had a couple of jobs and then I found work at The Rollin' Smoke."

"Joe Cabron's place?" Cam asked.

"Yeah. I started off at the bottom of the ladder and worked my way up." Vivi heard the note of pride in her voice and didn't give a damn. She'd badgered Joe to give her more work, more responsibility, a higher wage, and every task he gave her, she'd excelled at. And when she got to food preparation, they'd both realized with equal surprise that she had a natural affinity for flavors and a great cook's instinct. Together they'd played with recipes and food combinations, and when Joe decided to semi-retire, Vivi had gotten her chance at running his famous kitchen. Her appointment had sent shock waves through Houston's culinary circles, but she'd proved her worth—taking online courses to improve herself—and was now considered to be one of the best chefs in the city.

"I'm Joe's head chef."

Cam turned his head to look at her, his eyebrows raised. "You're kiddin'."

Vivi narrowed her eyes at him. "Please tell me that you aren't another Neanderthal man who thinks that only men should barbecue."

Cam's lips twitched. "Hell, I don't care who prepares my barbecue as long as it's done right. And at The Rollin' Smoke, it's done right."

Vivi nodded. "Damn straight." She started to pull her bottom lip between her teeth and remembered that she had a cut that needed healing. "I saw you there, at the restaurant, about three months back. You were eating lunch with Ryder Currin."

Cam nodded. "I eat with Ryder quite often and your place is one of our favorite places."

"I was in the kitchen and I saw you." She didn't tell him she'd felt like she'd been hit by a two-by-four, that her baby girl had been in the restaurant that day and he'd actually laid eyes on her before. Why complicate the story? "I asked who you were and then I did some research."

"What did you find out?"

"You're rich. You're successful. Along with Ryder Currin and Sterling Perry, you're considered to be one of the most influential businesspeople in Houston." Vivi picked at the rip in her jeans and stared out the window, idly noticing that they were just five minutes from her house. "It always worried me that Clem had no one, and if I died, she would become a ward of the state or, possibly worse, end up with my mother. I didn't know you, but I presumed that you would be a better option if something happened to me. So I listed you as my emergency contact, gave you custody of her in my will."

"And you didn't think that it might a good idea to tell me that I had a kid?"

She had, occasionally. But then she'd wavered, scared of the consequences. Because, while researching Cam, she'd discovered that the man was a control freak, a lone wolf, and that he rarely, if ever, sought business advice. It was his way, colleagues and associates were often quoted as saying, or the highway.

And that didn't work for her.

Cam pulled up to her sidewalk, parked and switched off the growly engine. Silence filled the car and Vivi slowly removed his sunglasses and carefully folded the arms.

"So why didn't you contact me when you found out who I was?" Cam asked.

Vivi placed the sunglasses on the lid of the console and met his eyes. She decided to tell him the truth, or some of the truth. "Because I knew that your coming into our lives would change it. And I like our life, I like what I've done with it."

Can rested his wrist on the steering wheel. "Change isn't always bad, Vivi."

Vivi opened the door, and when her feet touched the sidewalk, she looked back at him through the open car door. "No, it's not always bad but it's frequently hard. And messy."

* * *

Vivi's house was a small bungalow in a solidly middle-class area. Cam slammed his car door closed and looked up and down the empty street. It was early afternoon and the streets were deserted, with most people at work. But up and down the street, he could see signs that families lived here. A tricycle lay on the postage-stamp lawn belonging to Vivi's neighbor, a soccer ball rested against a rock next to the front door of the house opposite. Cam followed Vivi up the path to her front door and wondered how she was going to break into her own house, seeing that her house keys were probably somewhere in the Gulf of Mexico by now.

Vivi didn't miss a beat. She just lifted her mat, removed a brass key and inserted it into the flimsy lock on the front door. Seriously? Who did that anymore? In his previous life that would be the first place he'd look. "You have got to be kiddin' me."

Vivi frowned at him as she pushed open the front door and stepped inside the cool interior. "Problem?"

"I cannot believe you keep a front-door key under your mat. Have you heard about these characters called burglars? Rapists? Serial killers?" Cam demanded, shutting the door behind him and flipping the dead bolt. He saw her surprise and threw up his hands. "Please, please tell me that you lock your doors when you are here alone."

"It's a safe neighborhood."

Oh, God, that meant she didn't. Cam slapped his hands on his hips and closed his eyes, striving for calm. He knew it was a long shot, but it was worth a try, if only to get his blood pressure to drop. "You do have an alarm?"

"Nope."

"Mace? Pepper spray? A baseball bat?"

Vivi toed off her ruined sneakers and left them next to the door. Her feet were grubby, but he could still see the pale pink shade of polish on her toes. Sexy feet, he thought. He now remembered nibbling the arch of that elegant foot, and the way she'd shivered when he scraped his teeth against her skin.

Not important, he told himself, especially when she was living in a house a ten-year-old could break into. He'd need to get his security guy out here, to put a decent lock on all the doors and install an alarm. If he didn't, he'd never sleep again. Or he'd be bunking down on her couch every night.

Cam followed Vivi into a small living room containing two brightly covered sofas. A small TV sat on a wooden box and a bunch of bright flowers stood on a small table next to a bookcase. Cam narrowed his eyes and read the titles: a little romance, a lot of cookbooks, some true crime. He turned around slowly, saw the small dining table and, beyond it, a galley kitchen. A tiny pink handprint on a sheet of white paper was attached to the door of the fridge with a daisy magnet. He looked but he couldn't find any photos of her daughter—his daughter—anywhere.

"I was hoping to see a photo of Clementine."

"I normally have a bunch out but I'm having them reframed." Vivi's deep brown eyes, exhausted and full of pain, met his. "I have some on my phone." Then Cam caught the sheen of tears and watched as she swiped angrily at them. "Crap, no phone! My life is on my phone. My banking apps, my photos, my contacts, recipes… Everything."

Cam knew that the experiences of the day were coming back to pummel her, and she was fast running out of steam. She needed to shower and get some rest. He couldn't help but wonder if she'd ask him to buy her another phone, to lend her money to tide her over until she managed to get new bank cards. He wouldn't be surprised if she asked him to rent her a car or, hell, buy her one. He'd had girlfriends who thought sex gave them immediate access to his credit cards, so Vivi asking him for help wouldn't surprise him. But in this case, he'd give it. Clem was his daughter and there was no way he'd watch Vivi struggle when he could make her life easier.

And if he were the oil rigger he'd been years ago, if he'd been eating at The Rollin' Smoke as a normal guy at a normal table, drinking water instead of craft beer, would she still have tracked him down, found out who he was? How much of a factor was his money in Vivi's decision to name him as Clem's father, to list him as her go-to person? Would he be half so attractive without his money?

He didn't think so.

But instead of making demands, asking for help, Vivi walked into the kitchen and filled a glass with tap water. After drinking it down, she gripped the sink and gazed at the wall of her neighbor's house with a thousand-yard stare and panic-filled eyes.

To hell with it. She ought to be done with this day, with trying to remain strong, with attempting to keep it all together. He was taking over. Cam dumped his phone and wallet on the dining table and walked toward her. When he reached her, he bent his knees and scooped her up against his chest.

"What the hell, McNeal?"

Cam glared down at her. "Just for a second, stop thinking. Is Clem safe for a few hours?"

Vivi nodded. "Yes."

"Okay then." He walked into the hallway and nudged open the first door with his foot. A small bed, stuffed toys on the pillow, little girl shoes on the floor. Clementine's room and not what he was looking for.

"What are you doing?" Vivi demanded, her body stiff in his arms.

The bathroom was the next room and Cam walked inside and dropped Vivi onto the toilet seat. Ignoring her squawk, he flipped on the taps to the shower and met her angry glare. "Again, what the hell are you doing?" she demanded.

Cam squatted down in front of her, balancing on his toes. He rested his arm on his knee and met her eyes. "Vivianne, you've had a hell of a day. You had a close call, you are banged up and bruised. You're dealing with me, the father of your child, someone you didn't expect in your life. You have things to do and are facing a few uncomfortable days."

Vivi stared down at her hands and he saw her shoulders shake. Dammit, he was saying this wrong. He placed his hands on her thighs and tapped her thigh with his index finger.

"Look at me, Viv."

He waited until all that brown met his blue. "I'm here and as much as you want me to, I'm not going away. Not today."

Vivi stared at a point past his shoulder. "I can't… I'm not good at accepting help."

"I don't care. Today you're going to." Cam stood up and flipped the shower taps to maximum. "So, here's what's going to happen. You're going to shower and while you wash that river off you, I'll make you some tea, maybe something to eat. Then you're going to climb into bed."

Vivi shook her head. "I can't, Cam. I need to collect Clem, I need to find a phone, make arrangements for a car."

Stubborn had a new name and it was Vivi. "Yeah, you're not hearing me, Viv. I'm not going anywhere. For today, I'm your phone, I'm your lift, I'm the barrier standing between you and the outside world. I'm going to do whatever you need to do because you need to rest."

Vivi opened her mouth to argue, took a breath and slowly nodded. "I'll take two hours from you. Two hours and a cup of tea."

"Three hours, a cup of tea and a grilled cheese sandwich. And we'll pick up Clementine together."

Vivi shook her head. "I don't think I'm ready for that, Cam."

Cam lifted one shoulder and let it fall. "I don't think I am, either, but that's what's going to happen." He nodded at the shower before taking a step toward the door. Because the room was so damn small, one step was all it took to put him by the door. "Call if you need help."

"I won't."

Cam closed the door behind him and rested his forehead on the thin door. She acted so independent and determined, but was she really? Despite his so-called infallible BS detector, he had to wonder if he was reading her wrong. Was she just lulling him into a false sense of security, acting independent so that when she finally stung him, when she finally asked something of him, he wouldn't mind? Could she be that manipulative, that wily?

Yeah, he was cynical but he hadn't become that way by fluke and coincidence. And what was the point of worrying? He'd wait and see. Vivi would either disappoint him as so many had before her, or she'd surprise him. He'd expect the first and not hope for the second. That way he wouldn't feel let down.

Again.

Four

Three hours later, Vivi staggered out of her bed, thoroughly disoriented. Standing by the side of her bed, she stared out her window, surprised to see that the sun was still shining. She looked down at the pair of men's boxer shorts she'd pulled on and the thin tank top and wondered why she was dressed in her pj's in the middle of the afternoon. And why was it so quiet?

She had a toddler. Quiet was not good.

"Clem is safe, you're safe. Take a breath."

Vivi spun around and saw Camden McNeal standing in the doorway to her room, wearing designer jeans and a dark green T-shirt. His hair was shorter, there were fine lines around his eyes that hadn't been three years ago. And what was he doing in her house on a— God, what was today?

And where the hell was Clem?

Vivi lifted her hand to her throat, panic closing her throat.

"You had an accident. Clementine is fine. She's at the sitters. Charlie?"

Vivi sat down on the edge of the bed and dropped her head down, waiting for her dizziness to pass. Memories pieced themselves together. Near drowning, Cam as emergency contact, hospital, concussion. It was all coming back to her now. Blowing air out of her cheeks, she slowly lifted her head. "How long did I sleep for?"

"About three hours. I was just coming to wake you."

Vivi nodded her head and caught a glimpse of her reflection in the freestanding, secondhand mirror in the corner. She'd fallen asleep with wet hair and it was a mass of tangled, frizzy curls. She had a pillow crease on her left cheek, a bruise forming on her eyebrow, cheek and jaw. She was almost scared to look down, but she did. Black and blue with a few wonderful scrapes to break the monotony.

Because she wanted to cry—partly because she looked like hell in front of the ever-delicious-looking Camden McNeal—Vivi tried humor. "Holy crap. Clem is going to insist on kissing all these bruises better and that's going to take some time."

Cam pushed his broad shoulder into the door

frame and she saw the heat in his eyes. She glanced down and, yep, there was that telltale bulge behind the buttons of his jeans. "I'd be more than happy to take over when she gets tired."

He would, too. He'd be gentle with her, kiss her slowly, investigate every inch of her battered skin and then he'd caress her in such a way that she'd not only forget that she'd been in an accident but her own name. If they started tasting and touching each other, everything else would fade.

Vivi pulled her eyes away, tipped her head back and stared up at the ceiling. She couldn't go there, not with him. Their time to be lovers had passed. Now they had to find a new way of dealing with each other. A way that included Clem.

That was if Cam wanted to be part of Clem's life. She didn't even know. Right now, there were more important things to talk about, to figure out, than their crazy, combustible attraction.

Vivi gestured to her closet. "I'm going to get dressed and then maybe we can chat over a cup of coffee?"

Cam had the coffee ready when Vivi walked into her tiny, open-floor-plan living area ten minutes later. She'd changed into cutoff denims and flip-flops, pulling an open-neck, red-and-white-check shirt over her tank top and knotting it at the waist. Most of the bruises on her body were hidden and she'd toned down the ones on her face with some concealer. With her hair pulled back into a messy bun on the top of her head—her muscles ached too much to do anything more with the heavy mass—she felt 10 percent better and marginally human. She smiled her thanks at Cam as he pushed her coffee across the table.

"I left it black. That okay?"

"Sure."

Cam pulled out her chair and Vivi wasn't particularly surprised at his show of manners. Years ago, he'd opened doors for her, let her enter a room first. Held out chairs. Someone had drilled Southern manners into him somewhere along the way. Vivi watched as Cam took the chair opposite her, an unfamiliar laptop next to his elbow.

"That yours?" she asked, nodding to the state-of-the-art device.

A power cable snaked toward an electrical socket and a glass of water sat off to the right, next to a pile of folders. He'd arranged her small fan so that the air blew on him as he worked. She could see that all the windows to her small house were open. He'd also, at some point, sat on one of her small sofas—her cushions had been pushed to one end and a couple were on the floor. Cam McNeal had made himself very much at home in her space while she slept.

"Yeah," Cam replied, lifting his cup to his lips. "I managed to get some work done while you were sleeping. Do you feel better?"

Vivi considered his question. "I'm sore but I'm not feeling so…emotional."

"A near drowning will do that to you."

As will waking up and seeing the father of your child next to your bed. It was time to address the elephant in the room. "We need to talk about Clementine, Cam."

"Yeah."

She suspected that only pride kept him from squirming. Oh, he looked so inscrutable, so calm, but in the tapping of his finger against his coffee mug and the slight shift in his chair, Vivi saw that he wasn't quite as insouciant as he wanted to be.

"Let me tell you about Clem." Vivi wondered where to start and decided that there was no point in pussyfooting around. "She's strong-willed, bossy, demanding and energetic. She's amazingly bright." Vivi saw his skepticism and held up her hand. "I know, I sound like a doting mommy, but she genuinely is bright, and she has a hell of a vocabulary for her age. She must get that from you because I didn't really start speaking until I was four."

Mostly because her parents subscribed to the adage that children should be seen and not heard.

"She is just old enough to be excited about the idea of having a daddy but she's also only two, so the novelty will wear off in about two seconds," Vivi continued. She pushed her coffee cup away, rested her arms on the table and leaned forward. "You need to take some time to think about what your intentions are with regard to being Clem's dad, Camden."

Cam's amazing eyes narrowed. "What do you mean?"

"I mean you can't come roaring into her life and play at being her dad and then decide, in a few days or a few weeks, that it's not your thing. You can't pick her up and discard her."

Vivi rubbed the back of her neck. "Look, if you want to walk away, pretend this never happened, I'm okay with that. I'm not going to ask you for child support or anything like that."

Cam didn't speak. He just listened, his eyes locked on hers. Vivi touched the top of her lip with her tongue and forced herself to continue. This was difficult, but it needed to be said. Her little girl's heart was more important to her than her own.

"However, if you do decide you want to get to know her, we can arrange supervised visits. If those visits work out, I might then be open to allowing you time with her on your own. We'll have to see how it goes."

"Good of you," Cam said, his voice bland.

She didn't care if he was feeling insulted or annoyed; she had to do this. Vivi glanced at the clock on her wall, conscious of the hour. "Okay, it's time for us to leave."

She pushed her chair back and stood up. Knowing that it was always a good idea to step back, consider the options, she looked at Cam.

"I'm not going to tell Clem that you are her dad, not yet. Spend some time with her and then decide.

But you should know that if you make a promise to her, or to me about her, you *will* follow through. I will make sure of it."

He looked a little amused at the thought of her pushing him around but he'd yet to realize that when it came to Clem, there wasn't a mountain she wouldn't climb, a creature she wouldn't fight, a country she'd not invade. She was more than a momma bear, she was the whole damn pack.

Point made, Vivi thought, turning away. But as she was about to step out of the kitchen, he felt Cam's gentle hand gripping her elbow. *Don't turn around, Viv, because if you do, you know exactly what's going to happen.*

She turned anyway and got a hit of blue, the suggestion of amusement and the curve of a mouth before his lips covered hers. He tasted like before, like a wonderful memory, but also like someone new, a deeper and darker and more intense version of the man he used to be. And God, he felt hard and tough and solid. She didn't mean to lean into him but he easily accepted her weight, his one arm banding around her back in a hold that was both strong and reassuring. His other hand held her jaw, his fingers tracing the outline of her ear just as gently as his lips were exploring hers. It was a tender kiss, one she didn't expect, a "hello, it's nice to taste you again" kiss. But it wasn't enough. She didn't need gentle from Cam, or tender. She needed hot and hard and fast. She needed him to remind her that she was alive, that she was breathing, that she was young and…here, dammit.

Vivi grabbed his hips and pushed her breasts into his hard pecs, dragging her nipples across his chest. She opened her mouth and pushed her tongue past his teeth, needing to taste him, to explore and delve, to dip and dive. Heat and lust ricocheted through her and she felt her knees crumble, her bones melt. She was alive, she was kissing a sexy man, she was safe…

Vivi was unaware of tears rolling down her cheeks until Cam eased away from her and he wiped them away with his thumbs. He placed gentle kisses on the side of her mouth, her cheekbones, her temple, her forehead. "It's okay, Viv, you're safe. It's all good."

Oh, God. Vivi closed her eyes as Cam rested his head on her temple, his strong arms cuddling her close. He felt amazing and she hated the fact that she missed this…this *thing* she'd never had. Not him, pre-cisely, but what he represented: strength, support, someone in her corner.

But while it was nice, it wasn't something she could get used to, so Vivi tossed her head, stepped back and put a smile on her face and waved her hand in front of her face. "Sorry, delayed reaction to nearly dying."

"Understandable." Then Cam had the audacity to look amused. "But it could also be because you and I could still start a wildfire with the sparks we generate."

She was not going to encourage him, to respond to his sexy but smirky smile. "I nearly died. *That's* the only reason I kissed you."

Cam dropped his head and Vivi held her breath, waiting for his lips to meet hers again. She tipped her chin up and closed her eyes. Instead of his lips meeting hers, he murmured "BS" against her lips. Vivi jerked back and had to resist the urge to smack the smile off those sexy lips!

Gah!

And why was she still standing here, flip-flopping between smacking him senseless and kissing him stupid?

Cam pulled up to another house ten minutes from Vivi's and leaned across Vivi to open her door. His arm brushed her breast and he heard her intake of breath. Knowing that he couldn't look at her—if he did, he would crush his mouth to hers and nobody would be getting out of the car anytime soon—he pushed the door open and pulled back. She smelled incredible, of soap and shampoo and a scent that exuded her personality—forthright and clean, with a hint of spice.

Vivi released her seat belt and placed her hand on the door. She turned to face him, her eyes worried. "Maybe you should wait here. Charlie is a good friend, but I don't know if I'm up to explaining you just yet."

"If you had to, how would you explain me?"

Vivi released a laugh that was short on amusement. "I'd introduce you as the guy who seems to flip my world every time I run into him."

It was as good an explanation as any.

Cam watched Vivi walk up the path to the front door, hands in the back pockets of her cutoff denims. God, she was a spectacular-looking woman, but not in the rich-and-pampered way of the women he normally dated. Vivi was... What was the word he was looking for? She was *real*. Her hair was the same color it had been three years ago, a light brown with natural highlights. Her face was unpainted, those eyes lightening and darkening according to her mood. She was thinner than she'd been before, but all her curves were still there. And those legs, the ones that had gripped his hips as he slid into her, were still as jaw-droppingly shapely as ever.

His attraction to her burned brighter and hotter than before. Three years ago, he'd liked her—obviously. She'd been fun, a way to pass a couple of hours, a human connection. But this woman, the mother of the child he'd never known he had, well, she intrigued him. She'd just shared a little of her past, and he realized that there was a lot more to her story than she'd told him. Rising up through the ranks of a restaurant like The Rollin' Smoke wasn't something that happened on a routine basis, so she had to have talent as a chef as well as business savvy. And the fact that she'd had this meteoric career rise while raising a child floored him.

His phone buzzed. Cam looked at his display and hit the button to answer.

"Camden."

He smiled as Ryder Currin's deep voice rolled through his car. Ryder, who was a curious combination of big brother, favorite uncle and best friend, was one of the very few people Cam allowed to call him by his full name.

If Cam did everything he could to be unlike his dad or grandfather or any of his useless male ancestors, then Ryder Currin was the man he *did* try to emulate. Ryder was tough but fair, strong with a solid sense of community. Like Cam, he'd pulled himself up all by himself, for himself, and was now the majority shareholder in Currin Oil, his massive company headquartered in downtown Houston.

Ryder was also how Cam had gotten his start. Cam had heard of a small company needing $50,000 to stake a claim on a piece of land they were convinced held natural gas. Convinced they were on the right track, he had been prepared to risk his savings to invest but didn't have the entire amount. Or even half that. Taking a chance, he'd approached his then boss Ryder Currin, who had loaned him the money, asking very few questions. Three months later, the company had announced that they'd found one of biggest natural gas deposits in the country, and the find blew up their bank accounts. Well, maybe not Ryder's, who was already rich, but Cam's had certainly detonated.

Without that loan, Cam would not be living in River Oaks, driving a fancy car or operating a billion-dollar company. He owed Ryder: for his no-questions-asked faith in him, his continued friendship and for the ear he continued to provide.

"Any news on your missing kid?" Ryder asked.

God, he'd forgotten about Rick Gaines. But that was understandable, since the mother of his child had nearly died when her car ended up in a fast-flowing ditch and he'd discovered he had a daughter.

"Hold on a sec," Cam told Ryder and quickly accessed his messaging app. Scanning his messages, he found the one he was looking for and released a long sigh. Rick was found at a shelter and Cam passed the news along to Ryder.

"Talking about the missing, has the body at the TCC construction site been identified yet?"

"No. And Sterling Perry isn't talking, and neither are his people." Ryder remained quiet for a few moments before continuing. "By the way, Perry has called an emergency meeting of the TCC."

"Can he do that? The club isn't official yet—it hasn't been constituted. There haven't been any elections of officials, and a board hasn't been chosen. Have I missed something?"

"You missed nothing," Ryder growled, obviously pissed. "I am furious that Perry pulled rank and called this meeting. And to make his boardroom the venue? That's unacceptable."

Cam knew a little of Ryder's history with Sterling

Perry. Ryder had worked for Perry, who'd fired him for no cause. There were rumors that Ryder had an affair with Perry's wife, but Cam didn't believe that. Ryder wasn't the type to poach on another man's territory. What Cam knew for sure was that Ryder was left an oil-rich piece of land by Sterling's father-in-law and had built his massive empire on the oil he found on that land. Sterling, it was reported, had blown a gasket.

"So, are you going?" Cam asked. In the back of his mind he recalled an email about a TCC meeting but with the latest upheavals in his life—a daughter and her sexy, mind-blowing mother—TCC business had fallen way down on his list of priorities.

"I have no damn choice!" Ryder snapped back. "Everyone is going and I cannot afford to look petty. Especially since a representative from the state board of the TCC will be there."

"Must I be there to hold your hand?" Cam teased and grinned at Ryder's responding growl and muttered obscenity.

"I'm heading over there right now to give Sterling Perry a come-to-Jesus talk. In fact, I'm just pulling up to Perry Holdings now."

Crap. This wasn't going to end well. "Do you think that's a good idea?"

"Probably not," Ryder retorted. "But it will make me feel a lot better."

"Life is…complicated at the moment but I'll be at the meeting."

Ryder's voice dropped. "Are you okay, Cam?"

Cam hadn't intended to tell him, wasn't going to until the words flew out of his mouth. "I will be if you can tell me how to deal with having a baby daughter I never knew drop into my life. And how I should handle being reunited with a woman I've never quite forgotten."

Ryder chuckled. "Holy crap, Camden. That's huge. And, on one level, hilarious."

Except it really wasn't. It was his damn life.

"Angela?"

At the soft rap on her open office door, Angela Perry looked up to see Perry Holdings' receptionist standing in the doorway to her office. Pulling her attention from the report she'd been trying to digest, she waited for Andrea to speak.

"Ryder Currin is here, wanting to talk to your father."

Angela cursed as her heart took flight at the sound of Ryder's name. Ridiculous, really. "My father is out of town."

"I told him that but then he said he was sure you could take a message."

Angela rolled her eyes. This had to be about the meeting her father had, rather high-handedly in her opinion, called, inviting TCC Houston members. Or potential members. Her father really had to stop acting like he was president of the world. So, in fact, did Ryder Currin.

Too many men, Angela thought, standing up. Not enough aspirin.

The public area at Perry Holdings was a room full of men, and a few women, but Angela immediately found Ryder Currin. It was as if she held the receiver to a homing device pinned to his shirt. Angela looked down at her blue-and-white-striped dress and wondered if the tangerine jacket was too much. Irritated with herself—she always second-guessed her outfits because she wasn't quite as stylish as her twin, Miranda, nor as flashy as her best friend, Tatiana—she cursed her slightly damp palms and her accelerated heart rate. She was a shade off forty, dammit, a grown woman. Surely she shouldn't be feeling fluttery when she laid eyes on him.

"Mr. Currin, this way, please," Angela stated, happy to hear her voice sounded normal.

Ryder half smiled as his big stride ate up the space between them and Angela wished that she could step into his arms, lift her mouth for a kiss. She wanted this man, craved him with a passion that would make her father pop a vein.

"Can I help you?" Angela said, holding her hand out for him to shake. Ryder surprised her when he took her hand and dropped a kiss on her cheek. She inhaled his soap-and-sex scent and her head swam.

Perfect.

Ryder pulled her into the quieter hallway and his big hand cupped the side of her jaw. "I wanted to talk to Sterling but thought I'd also check in on you.

We had a pretty intense conversation about the past when we were together at the shelter."

Yeah, that conversation. The one where he told her that, contrary to what she'd always believed, he and her mother had never been anything but friends. Angela still wasn't sure whether she believed him or not. Oh, God, she wanted to, but a niggle of doubt remained. Okay, maybe more than a niggle.

"Why are you here, Ryder?" Angela asked, stepping back. "Oh, right, you want me to deliver a message to my father."

Ryder shook his head. "I'm more than capable of delivering my own messages to Sterling." He lifted a big shoulder and Angela wondered how his skin would feel, whether he'd taste as gorgeous as he looked. *Down, girl.*

"I just wanted to see you."

"There are these amazing things called phones and email." Angela pointed out, annoyed to hear that she was sounding breathless.

"Yeah, but that way I can't see you, smell you—" his voice turned rough, sexier "—kiss you."

Later she'd wonder what propelled her to act so out of character, to step up to him, to place her hands on his rough-with-stubble jaw and stand on her tiptoes to align her mouth with his. She felt his hands tighten on her biceps, and then his lips were under hers. Heat, lust and need shimmied over her and her tongue slipped between his open lips and into his mouth. God, he tasted like chocolate-covered sin. How had she lived for so long without kissing Ryder Currin?

She felt his hesitation, heard his silent "to hell with it" and then he took control of their kiss. His strong arm wound around her waist, pulling her up against his chest—and it was as hard as she'd imagined. He kissed her with assurance and confidence, like he knew exactly what she needed and how to give it to her. Angela teetered on her high heels but Ryder just tightened his grip on her.

"I've got you," he murmured against her open mouth. He hesitated, shrugged and dipped down again, and dialed the kiss up to hot and then to insane.

"Oops!"

Angela heard the feminine giggle and the masculine snort of laughter and yanked her mouth off Ryder's. She rested her forehead on his collarbone and tried to get her breathing under control. Dammit. The news that she'd kissed Ryder Currin—if such a tame word could be used to describe what they'd just done—would be all over the building in five minutes flat. God, she prayed that no one had the balls to tell her father.

Ryder's big hand skimmed down her back and rested on her hip. "I should go."

Angela nodded but didn't move. "Yeah."

Ryder's hand moved up and under her hair and he gripped the back of her neck. "This attraction between us is so damn unexpected."

Yeah. Unexpected and inconvenient. And messy. And liable to blow up in their faces.

But, Angela decided as she watched Ryder walk away from her, it was also the most excitement she'd had in *forever*.

TCC business and Ryder forgotten as he sat in his car, Cam banged his head against the headrest. He was attracted to Vivi's face and body, but he was also intrigued by her resilience, her strong spirit and her innate intelligence. Physical attraction was easy to ignore; mental attraction was hugely problematic. He didn't want to become emotionally entangled with Vivi. He couldn't afford the distraction. He needed to focus on his company, his career, on becoming the success he wanted to be.

You are already successful, he heard Ryder's voice say in his head. *How much money is enough? When are you going to be satisfied with how far you've come and finally be proud of your achievements?*

Cam didn't know. He just knew that he wasn't there yet.

He closed his eyes, remembering his father tossing out his newest plan, his latest scheme to make money. None were legal, and none made money. Jack had no qualms about ripping off an elderly lady of her savings, stealing the social security checks of unemployed mothers and forging their signatures. Breaking into houses with his son to scoop up anything that he could flip for a profit.

Yet, despite their many scores, their standard of living had never changed. They still bounced from crappy apartments to squats to rented rooms; Cam still wore clothes that were too small and was constantly expected to miss school to pick pockets so he could feed himself and his father.

Would life have been better if his mother had stuck around? From what he'd heard about her, probably not. Fantastic genes he'd passed on to Clementine.

Cam gripped the steering wheel to anchor himself. How could he ever tell Vivi, and eventually Clementine, that his parents lived on the fringes of society, that they'd been criminals and cons? God, he should drive away, stay out of their lives.

He might have money and respect but it didn't change the fact that he was a product of the streets, the son of two people who had all the education and impulse control of a puppy. He didn't have a nurturing bone in his body because he'd never been nurtured. How could he be the father Clem deserved?

Terrified of being a dad and of Vivi finding out about his past, Cam touched the ignition button with his index finger. He was about to start the car when the front door of the house opened and Vivi stepped onto the porch, a little girl on her hip. Cam dropped his hands and stared, his heart bouncing off his rib cage.

God, she looked like him, a feminine version of the child he'd been. Her hair, held in two high pigtails, was the same color as his when he'd been a child, a lighter shade of brown than it was now. She had his nose, his chin and, yeah, his light blue eyes. She had Vivi's fine, dark eyebrows and long lashes and her mouth, but essentially she was a McNeal.

Cam was vaguely aware that Vivi was talking to her sitter, saw hugs and kisses being exchanged, but he couldn't keep his eyes off Clem. This was his kid. His DNA had helped formed her, his blood flowed in her veins. She was his.

Even if he wanted to, he couldn't walk away. Because how did one walk away from love at first sight?

Five

Please let him like her...
   Please don't let this be weird...
   Please let me do and say the right thing...
   Conscious of Clem's chattering in her ear—
something about Charlie and a cake—Vivi pulled
in a deep breath and watched Cam exit his car and
walk around the hood to meet them on the sidewalk. Vivi had always thought that Clem looked
like Cam, but now she noticed how close the resem-
blance was. Vivi stopped a yard from him and met
his eyes, suddenly tongue-tied. She wanted to hold
Clem out to him, wanted to show her off like a toy.
*Look what I made. See what I did. Don't you think
I did a good job?*

Cam's eyes, deeper and more intense, bounced between her and Clem, and a small smile touched his lips. He jammed his hands into his pockets, and Vivi saw him swallow and heard him clear his throat. "She's—" he hesitated "—she's beautiful, Vivi."

Vivi turned her head to look into Clem's curious eyes, brushing the back of her hand across her cheek. "She really is."

Clem, suddenly noticing her mother's cuts and scrapes, placed both her hands on Vivi's cheeks and stared at her. "Owie, Mommy?"

"Not so bad, sweetheart," Vivi told her.

"Kiss better?" Clem asked.

"Absolutely."

Vivi closed her eyes as Clem's small lips gently kissed her cut, then her scrape and her bruise. Vivi thanked her and squeezed her, her love for this child threatening to drop her to her knees.

"Where Mommy car?" Clem asked, looking from Cam to his big car.

"My car isn't working," Vivi told her, hitching Clem's bag up higher on her shoulder. She smiled her thanks when Cam slid the bag off her shoulder and easily held it in one hand. Right, time to get this done. "Clem, this is Cam. He's going to take us home."

Clem sent Cam a frank look, tipping her head to one side and taking her time to decide whether to greet him or not. When she hid her face in Vivi's neck, Vivi knew that she was feeling uncharacteristically shy.

She patted Clem's back. "Honey, do you want to say hi to Cam?"

Cam shook his head. "Don't force it, Vivi. She'll say hello when she's ready."

Surprised by his sensitivity, Vivi thanked him as he opened the rear passenger door. She automatically turned to put Clem into her car seat and it took her a moment to realize that there *was* a car seat, in *his* car.

"You got a car seat. For Clem."

Cam shrugged. Well, yeah. Because she was a kid and kids needed to be protected. Work wasn't all he'd done while she was sleeping, he wanted to tell her.

"Uh, thank you?" Vivi said, obviously surprised.

Vivi's astonishment annoyed Cam. He could be considerate, capable of thinking of someone other than himself, and he would never do anything to harm a child.

Cam walked around the car, climbed inside and looked at the child sitting behind his passenger seat. She looked so much like him it was scary. Clem returned his frank assessment, and when a tiny smile touched her pretty mouth, he felt like she'd hit him with a two-by-four.

"Would you have ever told me about her?" he quietly asked when Vivi took her seat.

He felt Vivi tense. This was a question she didn't want to answer but...tough.

"Well?" he demanded when she didn't speak.

"Probably not," Vivi answered.

When she didn't expand, he turned his head and nailed her with a hard look. "Why not?"

"Because I like making decisions on my own, not having anyone to answer to. Involving you in her life would've made my life complicated and I don't do complicated. I like being independent and I like being on my own."

Truth coated every word she uttered and blazed from her eyes. Her warning—*I will never be controlled by you or anyone else*—could've been on a twenty-foot billboard and it still wouldn't be clearer than these quietly uttered words in his car.

Keep your distance, Cam.

Let me go back to my life, Cam.

Roll back the clock.

Cam rolled his head to look at her fully and their eyes connected, heat and want and desire arcing between them. He knew her brain wanted her to be sensible and distant but he also knew her body wanted what his did. To get naked as soon as possible. He wanted to taste those lips, explore her body, taste every inch of her creamy skin.

He also wanted to delve into that sharp brain, peek behind those walls she'd so carefully erected and reinforced.

He was looking for trouble. And couldn't wait to find it.

Vivi sighed when Cam parked his car in the driveway to her small red brick cottage. Fumbling with the clasp of her seat belt, she felt Cam's fingers on hers and silently cursed when lust skittered over her skin and flashed through her body. She'd had a hell of a day, so why was her battered body responding like this? Their earlier kisses she could put down to adrenaline and delayed reaction but she couldn't keep using those excuses. How could she, after a near-death experience, be feeling…well, horny? Sure, Cam was a great-looking guy with the ability to set female hormones on fire, but after everything that had happened today, shouldn't she be immune?

Vivi lifted her eyes to meet his and saw heat in the blue depths, heard his intake of breath, noticed the slight flush on his cheekbones. Dammit. He was feeling it as well.

Vivi pulled her bottom lip between her teeth and closed her eyes. She pulled her hand out from under his and the seat belt released with a soft snick. It was time to pull herself back to real life, to find some sort of stable ground. Yeah, she'd had a crap day, but it was over, and she needed a reset.

Except that she had a feeling Cam wasn't going to cooperate and allow her life to go back to normal. Vivi sighed and pushed her hair off her forehead. But after a day like today, how could anything be normal again?

Vivi felt Cam's thumb skate over her cheekbone. "Let's get you inside, sweetheart."

Vivi turned her head to look at him, her limbs feeling as heavy as steel girders. The soft, sweet-sounding word became deeper and sexier when he uttered it in his growly, deep voice. She liked hearing it…

But she had to remind herself that men like Cam—good-looking men who could be charming—knew how to turn it on. He was a Texan, and men like him knew how to use *sweetheart* and *darlin'* to maximum effect. It was practically part of the Southern boy's school curriculum.

"Let's get you and the half-pint inside," Cam said before leaving the car. Vivi waited for him to walk around his car to open her door—Texas manners again—and swung her legs around to place her feet on the footboard. Her body ached, her muscles moaned and the ground seemed like a long way down. She was sore, she was tired and all she wanted to do was to sleep.

Nearly dying had wiped away all her strength. Go figure.

Then Vivi felt Cam's hands on her waist, and with no effort at all, he lifted her up and out of the car, and lowered her gently. Keeping his arm around her waist, he tipped her chin up. She caught the concern in his face. And, yep, under the concern, desire flashed. "You okay?"

She wanted to tell him she was worried that if he let her go, her knees would buckle and, worse, she would burst into tears. She nearly told him she was exhausted, that she didn't think that tonight she was up to being the mommy Clem needed and deserved. That she needed, just this once, to have someone else's hands on the wheel.

Vivi dropped her eyes and sighed. She hauled back the words hovering on the tip of her tongue, swallowed them down. She would never, ever give anyone an inch of control. Because she knew that land surrendered could never be reclaimed. Her mom, her home, her church were all gone. She'd learned that lesson well.

"Thanks for the lift." Vivi stepped away from Cam, putting a whole bunch of space between them. "I'll just grab Clem and we'll get out of your hair."

His eyes moved from her face to Clem, who was still in her car seat, softly singing. When Cam looked back at Vivi, he shook his head before lifting his hand to encircle her neck. Vivi wanted to pull away, but because Cam's fingers were kneading the tension out of her muscles, she just sighed and released a small groan of pleasure.

Then Cam's head dipped down and he used his thumb to tip up her jaw. His breath was the only barrier between their lips and then there was nothing but his mouth on hers. Vivi felt her body sag, her knees buckle, and was grateful when Cam banded his arm around her back, taking her weight.

So good, Vivi thought, as his mouth moved over hers. Strong and masculine and assured and confident. Cam's tongue slipped between her lips, gently demanding entrance. She shouldn't, she really shouldn't, but her lips were suddenly operating independently of her brain. She needed this, needed him to kiss her in the sunshine of a balmy, late afternoon. She'd take his kiss, suck up his strength, borrow some of his confidence and then she'd send him on his way.

She just needed this minute, and maybe one or two more.

Cam's hand slid down her back, his thumb tracing her spine. He then splayed his hand on her lower back, his fingers cupping her butt. He pulled her in and Vivi felt the ridge in his jeans as his erection pushed into her stomach. Pleasure, at both his response and at the fact that she could make this gorgeous man so hard, so quickly, rushed through her. Vivi gripped his shirt just above his belt, telling herself that she couldn't, shouldn't touch him, that she couldn't take him in hand.

They were outside her house, she had nosy neighbors, and her child was not a few feet from them.

Vivi twisted his shirt tighter, unable to stop herself from rocking into him, from winding her tongue around his, from moaning in the back of her throat. The heat he generated was insane; the need he dragged to the surface held the same power of the recent storm.

He was a perfect package of power and destruction in six foot something of sexiness.

But while climatic events were powerful and breathtaking, they were also destructive and damaging. They were, as she very well knew, to be avoided. So Vivi placed her hand flat against Cam's chest and pushed him away. He muttered a curse, reaching for her again, but Vivi quickly stepped back, shaking her head. No, it was time to be sensible, way past time to shut this down. After rubbing her hands over her face, she pushed past Cam to open the back door. Seeing Clem's face settled her, reminded her that she was a mommy first, a chef second, and that she had no time for kissing sexy men in the sunshine.

She had no business kissing Cam, her one-night stand.

And the father of her beautiful, smart kid.

Vivi flipped open the car seat clasp and winced when Clem tumbled into her jellylike arms. Grimacing, she settled Clem on her hip and reached for the bag Cam had placed on the floor below Clem's feet. Her back muscles screamed as she bent down, her fingertips brushing over the handle of the bag. Dammit, she was stiffening up. She reached for the bag again and this time she couldn't stop a low groan from leaving her mouth. She couldn't help looking at Cam, hoping that he hadn't heard. He was standing behind her, his arms crossed, his legs slightly apart. His head was cocked, and his expression inscrutable, but she recognized the frustration and annoyance in his eyes.

"Are you done being a stubborn ass?"

Vivi narrowed her eyes at him but swallowed down her hot retort. "Thanks for the lift. It was…" She hesitated, looking for the right word. Amazing?

Great? Exciting? Knee-collapsing? "…interesting seeing you again," she finished.

Cam had the nerve to grin. "Do you really believe that I am just going to be a good boy and ride away?"

No, of course, she didn't. She wasn't that naive. Or stupid. "One could hope," Vivi muttered. She shifted Clem on her hip, wondering when her daughter had picked up another twenty pounds.

"Good try but…no." Cam lifted his hands and looked Clem in the eye, silently asking her whether he could carry her. Clem shocked her by leaning forward with a sunny grin. Two seconds later, she was perched on Cam's thick forearm, two sets of identical blue eyes looking at her. Vivi stepped forward, wanting to take her back, needing to regain control of the situation. Then Clem dropped her head and rested her temple against Cam's collarbone, fully comfortable being held by this strange man.

Vivi couldn't blame her. Cam exuded capability and confidence, and babies were barometers. Cam made her and, apparently, her daughter feel secure, like he was the barrier that stood between them and an ugly world.

Vivi felt a burning sensation in her eyes and cursed the tears blurring her vision. That was her job; she'd been that person for Clem all her life! How could Cam stride into their lives and just take over? It wasn't right, and it wasn't fair!

But as she knew, so much about life wasn't fair.

Cam gently pushed her away from the door and

reached down and snagged Clem's bag. He closed the back door and transferred the bright pink bag to his other hand. Then Vivi's hand was swallowed by his and she immediately felt calmer, as if the earth had stopped rocking beneath her feet. Like Clem, she couldn't help responding to his strength and his capability.

As they walked to the front door of her cottage, Vivi tried to convince herself to put her foot down, to tell him to leave. But she was utterly exhausted, and the words wouldn't come.

Pulling her house key out of the back pocket of her cutoffs she tried to open the door, silently cursing when she missed the lock. Cam didn't say anything but just took the key from her hand, jammed it in the lock and opened the door for her. And as Vivi stepped into her house—the home she'd made for her and her daughter—she told herself that it was okay to lean, just for a half hour, maybe a little more.

She'd take a little time to gather her strength and her courage and then she'd send Cam on his way. She didn't need him.

She just needed her daughter.

Cam, with Clem still in his arms, stepped into the hallway of Vivi's small house, grateful for the cool, fragrant air. The house held that perfectly pleasant smell that only came with the presence of females—perfume and powder, sweet and sexy. Cam placed his hand on Clem's small back, his eyes moving from Vivi's face to his daughter's, thinking that his life had been woman free—casual sexual encounters couldn't be counted—and now he had two girls who'd dropped into his life.

And despite Vivi's not-so-subtle go-away attitude, he intended to keep them there. Being part of Clem's life was a no-brainer; he fully intended to be her dad, however bad he might be at it. But he could learn, he would learn. He had no intention of being the same waste-of-space parent his father had been.

He heard Clem's sigh and looked down to see her long eyelashes against her cheeks, her tiny hand on his chest. She suddenly felt a little heavier, her breathing a little deeper. She was, he realized, asleep. His mouth tipped up in a wry smile: at least someone in this house trusted him.

Vivi, who obviously had a finely tuned mom radar, lifted her head. Her expression softened as love, pure and incandescent, turned her dark eyes liquid. He'd never seen so much love in one expression, and his cold, hard heart rolled around his rib cage. His daughter was deeply loved, and Cam's throat clogged with gratitude. He was pissed at Vivi's secretiveness, confused by her reluctance to contact him, discombobulated by her sudden and dramatic reappearance in her life and kicked off-kilter by his raging attraction to her.

But beside all that, he was fundamentally and completely grateful that she loved his daughter.

Not all mothers did.

Cam looked away from her, hoping she hadn't noticed his emotional reaction. He didn't know how to deal with these complicated feelings and he certainly couldn't discuss them.

"She normally goes down for a nap around about now," Vivi said. "I'll go put her down and then I'll walk you to your car."

Did she really think she'd get rid of him that easily? Vivi reached for Clem but Cam shook his head. "I've got her."

Vivi looked like she was wanted to argue, but instead she just shrugged and walked away. Cam followed her through the living room. Her house was nothing like his exquisitely decorated mansion in River Oaks; it could probably fit into one wing of his stupidly big residence. But every inch was warm and welcoming and personal. This was Vivi and Clem's space; they lived here. Unlike him, who just seemed to inhabit his house.

If the choice was between luxury and warmth, space and coziness, Vivi's house would win hands down. It was a home, while his place was just a richly decorated space.

Vivi opened the door to the small bedroom and gestured him inside. There were stuffed animals in Clem's bed, and the curtains were printed with tiny farm animals. A chest of drawers stood in the corner of the room and a battered bookcase held a wide variety of children's books.

Cam's attention was pulled from the room when

Vivi bent over to toss the stuffed animals to the bottom of Clem's bed. God, she had a perfect ass. His eyes drifted down and Cam could easily imagine those long legs wrapped around his waist, her breasts in his hands, her sexy mouth on his. God, he wanted her. As much—no, far more than he had three years ago.

Vivi straightened and turned, and their eyes collided. Moments passed as electricity arced between them, and neither of them moved, each knowing that the other was remembering, wanting, craving. Memories of that night occasionally surfaced, along with mild regret, and he accepted that making love with Vivi was one of the best sexual experiences of his life. But Cam knew that if he made love to her now, tonight, nothing would ever be the same.

It was almost enough to make him walk away. If it weren't for Clem, he would.

Vivi wrenched her eyes away and gestured to the bed. "You can just lay her down. She won't wake up. She sleeps like the dead."

Cam stepped up to the bed and Vivi moved away, as if scared to touch him. He didn't blame her; they had the ability to go up in flames. He held Clem gently, releasing his breath when she was on the bed, her cheek on her pillow. Vivi, still taking care not to make contact, tugged her tiny shoes off her feet and then her socks, revealing perfect, perfect toes. Everything about Clem was perfect…

And Clem's mommy wasn't too bad, either.

Vivi placed the shoes and socks on top of the chest of drawers, crossed her arms and rocked on her heels. "So, again, thanks for your help. But if you don't mind, I'd like you to leave."

He wasn't ready for go, not yet. He could stay here. This could be his place.

Cam closed his eyes and shook the fantasy away. *Just because you have a daughter doesn't mean you have a family. It doesn't work like that. Not now, not ever. You're projecting, fantasizing, McNeal. That isn't something you do, something you're allowed to do.*

You deal in facts, cold and hard.

Cam jammed his hands into his pockets, his eyes on Vivi's extraordinarily lovely face. *So, deal in the cold and the hard*, he told himself.

He wanted Vivi. Wanted her more than he wanted to take another breath.

He wanted to be part of Clem's life. He would be part of her life.

And that meant not allowing Vivianne to hustle him out of her house, her life. That meant sticking. And staying.

Cam tipped his head, considering a plan of action. He could seduce Vivi. It wouldn't be hard. She wanted him as much as he wanted her. Within a minute, maybe two, they would be swept away by lust and need and want, oblivious to anything but how they made each other feel. It would be easy, effective, efficient.

But sometimes easy and effective wasn't right, wasn't honorable. Vivi had had a hell of day and she looked wrung out. He knew that she was physically sore, bruised and battered, and she had to be as confused and wary about his reappearance in her life and Clem's as he was about her.

And he wanted Vivi willing and eager and hot and wild. He wanted her fully engaged, utterly focused on him and how he made her feel. He wanted all of her, every lovely mental and physical inch of her.

He should leave, give her some space, but he didn't want to. Not yet. But he didn't have a good enough reason to stay.

"It's been a crazy day, huh?"

Cam released a quick laugh at her understatement. "Crazy is one word for it," he admitted, pushing his hand through his hair. Suddenly noticing that his throat was dry, he gestured to the door. "Got anything to drink? I'm parched."

Vivi wrinkled her nose, as if trying to remember what was in her fridge. "I have some white wine… Maybe a beer?"

"Beer would be good," Cam replied. He sent Clem another look—God, he had a daughter!—and followed Vivi down the hallway and toward the kitchen. He leaned against the counter and crossed his legs at the ankles, watching as her head disappeared into the fridge, leaving him with a view of that ass and those legs again.

Cam rubbed his hand over his face and forced his

thoughts out of the bedroom. God, he hadn't thought this much about sex and a woman's body since he was sixteen. *Time to get a grip, McNeal.* And maybe, dammit, it was time for him to go.

He could pick this up tomorrow, the day after… Maybe he should give himself, and Vivi, some time to come to terms with this turn-their-lives-upside-down day.

Vivi straightened and closed the fridge door before spreading apart her empty hands. "Sorry, no beer. And my wine is also finished."

Cam suspected that she was lying and that like him, she'd had a bit of a talk to herself while her face was buried in the fridge. He didn't like lies—couldn't stand them, in fact—but he'd let this one slide. "No problem." He stood up straight and pulled his car keys from his back pocket. "Can I do anything else for you before I go?"

Surprise flashed across Vivi's face, suggesting that she wasn't used to offers of help. And that pissed him off. Where were her friends? Her family? "Do you want to use my phone to call anyone for you? Your mom, a friend?"

Distaste jumped in and out of her eyes and her expression cooled. "No, thank you. I'm perfectly fine on my own."

And he thought he was proud and self-sufficient. Miss Vivianne almost had him beat. "You sure?" he pushed.

"Very." Vivi snapped out the word.

Whoa, fierce. Cam lifted his hands, a little amused. His daughter's mom had fire in her veins and he liked that, liked that she wasn't a pushover, that she was independent and feisty. God help him when he got her back into bed. They'd both spontaneously combust.

Because that was exactly where they were going,

And if he didn't leave this house right now, that was going to happen sooner than later...

Cam heard the discreet beep from his phone and pulled the device from his back pocket. Like many other Houstonians, he'd set up a series of alerts on his phone to keep abreast with the flood situation. Now he was suddenly glad he had. He read the Tweet once, then again, just to make sure before releasing a quick, sharp curse.

Vivi snapped her head up, immediately realizing that something was very wrong. "What is it?"

"Water has spilled over the wall of the Addicks Reservoir, and the Barker Reservoir is very close to its limits. The Army Corps of Engineers are going to open the gates to the reservoirs. A mandatory evacuation order has been issued. You need to get out of here."

Vivi just stood there, her forehead wrinkling. "But those reservoirs are supposed to help with the flooding."

"I think they are in a 'damned if you do, damned if you don't' situation," Cam replied. "But we don't have time to argue about the pros and cons of the engineers' decisions, Viv. Your house could be flooded. I need to get you and Clem out of here. Let's go."

Vivi nodded and all but ran out of the room, Cam hot on her heels. "Can you grab Clem while I pack a bag?"

Cam grabbed her arm and spun her around. "We don't have time for you to grab anything, Viv, except Clem. We have to go now!"

"Some toiletries, a change of clothing," Vivi protested.

Because he understood how hard it was to walk away from everything you'd struggled to earn, he wanted to give her that time, but her life and Clem's were far more important than clothes and things. He forced himself to ignore her pleading eyes, her sad expression. "Clem. That's it."

He didn't give her a chance to answer, spinning on his heels to return to Clem's bedroom. Gathering her in his arms, he released a frustrated grunt when Vivi darted past him to pick up a stuffed monkey toy, well-loved and battered. He tasted panic in the back of his throat, not knowing how much time they had. Holding Clem against his shoulder, he grabbed Vivi's hand and tugged her through her house. He ushered Vivi into the front seat and took a moment to place Clem in her car seat, quickly figuring out the clasp that held her in place. She was still asleep, thank God. A screaming, crying child would make this situation that much worse.

Running around the hood of his car, he noticed that the neighborhood was suddenly alive with activity. A car farther up the street was pulling out, another on its tail.

This wasn't a drill, this was real life and it was as scary as hell. Would he be this worried if he was only worried about his own hide? Probably not. Being responsible for Vivi, and Clem, increased his anxiety by a thousand degrees.

He would not let anything happen to them…

Starting the SUV, Cam pulled out of the driveway. He stomped his foot on the accelerator as his eyes flicked between his rearview mirror, the road in front of him and his speedometer. He grimaced as he geared down, taking the corner on something that was close to two wheels.

Thank God that catching drivers speeding through a residential area was the last thing on the minds of cops this afternoon.

Six

She'd trashed her car, nearly drowned, been admitted into the ER unconscious and forced out of her house thanks to a dam overflowing. And Cam Mc-Neal was back in her life. It was fair to say she'd had a hell of a day. So when Cam pulled into the super exclusive neighborhood of River Oaks and then into the circular driveway of a French-château-inspired home, Vivi didn't have any energy left to feel surprised.

She glanced into the back seat, saw that Clem was still asleep and looked past the house to the golf course that formed the back border to his house. She couldn't imagine Cam playing golf, schmoozing it up with his business buddies on the links. Despite his designer clothes and luxury car, Cam looked too wild for the preppy sport. With his height and build she could see him playing rugby or water polo, hard, intense sports that required strength and stamina, determination and aggression.

Following a small ball across acres of grass didn't seem his style.

But what did she know? She'd spent a night with the man three years ago; she'd barely scratched the surface of what made Cam tick. Vivi gestured to the golf course. "Do you play?" she asked, her curiosity demanding an answer.

Cam dropped his big hands from the wheel—long fingers, wide hands, hands that had caressed her with a skill she'd never known before or since—and released a short, sharp chuckle.

"Ryder Currin has pulled me onto the links more times than I'd like, and I hated every moment. He calls me a ham-handed philistine." Vivi caught the note of affection in his voice for Ryder. Ryder, as she'd read, had been Cam's first investor, and from their visits to The Rollin' Smoke, she knew they were good friends. But the admiration and respect she heard in Cam's voice, conveyed in only a few words, suggested he was more than Cam's good friend and that there was a bond between them that went deeper than she'd suspected. Vivi wanted to pry and probe but forced herself to pull the words. The world had shifted under her feet a few times today. She didn't need to complicate her life further by digging into Cam's fascinating inner world.

And dammit, every aspect of him was fascinating. He was rough and tough and acerbic and controlling, but underneath it all he was also kind and considerate and generous. She didn't know what to make of him. On her best day—and today was very far from being that—she'd find him challenging. He was still in top physical shape, but he felt harder, stronger, more capable than three years ago, more solid, like his feet were firmly anchored to the earth.

So were hers, Vivi admitted. They'd both come a long way in three years. They'd both worked their tails off, and while she wasn't as financially fluid as Cam—few people were—she was proud of how far she'd come.

She was also proud of her child's dad for what he'd accomplished. If only he still wasn't so damn sexy, if only he still didn't affect her. One look from him and she melted, envisioning him undressing her, those big hands skimming her body, his talented fingers finding her secret, long-neglected places, his mouth devouring hers. She still wanted him.

She really didn't want to want him.

Cam's gentle touch, his fingers brushing her hand, pulled her back to the present, and she realized that she'd been staring at him. Vivi felt her cheeks heat. "Are you okay?" Cam asked, his rough voice full of concern. How many times had he asked her that today? Far too many.

She had a damn good excuse for her inattention and she'd use it. After all it wasn't every day that one could claim to have cheated death. "It's been a long, tough day."

"That's an understatement."

And as much as she wanted to fall face-first into a bed, she had a child to look after, to feed and bathe, who needed love and attention. And she could do that someplace else. She couldn't stay here with Cam. It was all too much. "Can you take me to a hotel, Cam?"

Cam turned in his seat, rested his wrist on the steering wheel and sighed. "If I make you feel that uncomfortable, I'll drive you two blocks over and book you into one of the guest suites of the country club. At my cost."

"I can pay—" Then Vivi realized that she couldn't actually pay for a damn thing. Her purse containing her identification and her bank cards was long gone.

"Look, why not just stay with me? I have guest bedrooms. My housekeeper will be in in the morning and since she routinely moonlights as a nanny to some of the neighborhood kids, she'll be more than happy to help me keep an eye on Clem if you want to sleep in or just take a break." Cam turned his eyes from her face to look at his enormous house. "You'll be safe here, and Clem will be safe here. Isn't that the most important thing right now?"

He used the one argument she didn't have a rebuttal for. Clem's safety would always be her top priority. Vivi ran her fingers across her forehead. She wanted to tell him she was scared, that she felt uncomfortable being here with him. She was terrified he would be too good to them, that she would find herself falling under his spell, swept away by the fantasy of playing a happy family with the wealthy, sexy father of her child. Cam was magnetic and her desire for him hadn't faded; she could easily imagine herself in this house, in his bed.

But Cam was a take-no-prisoners, my-way-or-the-highway type of guy, and she would never, ever allow him that amount of control over her or Clem. It was her life, and Clem was her daughter; she would sink or swim by her choices.

"I'm not asking you to marry me or to move in, Vivianne," Cam said, sounding impatient. "It'll just be for a few days, until you can return to your house."

Vivi narrowed her eyes at him. "So you aren't intending to seduce me, to find a place in my—Clem's life?"

Cam flashed her a quick, rakish smile. "Of course, I am. Our chemistry is off the charts. And Clem is my daughter, so of course, I want to get to know her. But that doesn't necessarily translate into marriage and moving in. Besides, I'm not cut out for family life in suburbia."

Vivi looked from him to his big house with its elegant facade, sparkling windows and beautifully landscaped gardens. Raising both eyebrows, she said,

"Then why the hell do you own this house in the trendiest suburb in Houston?"

Cam turned away from her, muttered something that sounded like "I have no damned idea" before tapping a button on his dashboard. The massive garage door opened and he drove his SUV into the garage. Vivi looked at the expensive super-bike, the powerful boat and a German-engineered, imported sports car and shook her head.

She'd come a long way in three years—from broke and pregnant to stable and successful—but Cam's success had been meteoric. Vivi looked behind her and smiled at her daughter's peaceful, beautiful face. Cam had the money but she had Clem.

She'd got the better deal, no doubt about it.

"Shh, Clem, Mommy might still be sleeping."

"I is hungry."

Vivi, half asleep, wanted to tell Cam that nobody came between Clem and her food, but her eyelids felt heavy and the words stuck in her throat. She sighed and pushed her head into the soft down pillow, allowing her body to sink into the super comfortable bed.

Vivi felt the tiny hand patting her face. "Mommeee! I's hungry!"

"I'm sure I have cereal, Clem. Let's leave Mom to sleep and see what we have."

Clem asked if he had a particularly sugary cereal that wasn't standard fare in their household, and Vivi realized that sometime between yesterday and this morning, Clem had lost her shyness and was her normal chatty self.

"Your teeth will fall out, Clementine, if you eat that rubbish," Vivi mumbled, still unable to lift her heavy lids.

Clem rested her lips on hers and Vivi smiled. Early-morning kisses from Clem were just the best thing ever. She opened her eyes and smiled. "Hey, baby girl. Did you have a good sleep?"

Clem nodded enthusiastically. "I trieded to wake you."

Bad Mommy. Vivi pushed away the surge of guilt and stroked Clem's cheek. "Sorry, baby. Give me ten minutes and we'll make a plan for breakfast."

"Am going to Charlie?"

Vivi forced herself to think. What was today? Friday? No, it was Saturday and that meant no day care. And because she had Clem with her, that also meant she couldn't go down to The Rollin' Smoke to help clean up the restaurant. But maybe they could take a drive down there and see if any progress had been made.

Then she remembered that she didn't have a vehicle. Or a phone to arrange for one. Or identification.

"No, Clem, you're going to stay with me today."

Clem smiled and Vivi saw her dimple, the flash of mischief in her smile. Her daughter was going to be a handful when she was older and Vivi was going to have to become a lot smarter. But not today. Today she just wanted to go back to sleep. But she couldn't.

She was a single mom and single moms couldn't take the day off.

"I heard there was a little girl in the house. I wonder if she likes pancakes."

Vivi frowned at the lilting Irish brogue and her eyes darted to Cam's, silently asking for an explanation. Having Cam see her sleepy, mussed and rumpled was one thing. Meeting a total stranger in one of Cam's T-shirts and with messy hair was not going to happen. She turned over to sit up and released a sharp hiss as her muscles protested, volubly reminding her that she'd tangled with a ravine and water and nearly lost.

"That's my housekeeper, Sally. She loves kids and she makes the best pancakes ever." Cam held out his hand to Clem and Clem immediately ran to him, sliding her hand into his, apparently without a second thought. They stepped into the hallway and Vivi listened as Cam introduced Clem to his housekeeper.

"You don't look like a girl who likes pancakes." Sally said.

"I does, I like them lots!" Clem immediately responded.

"How many can you eat?" Sally asked and Vivi liked the way she spoke to Clem.

"A hundred!" Clem proclaimed. Vivi rolled her eyes at her daughter's pronouncement. A hundred seemed like a good number to a two-year-old.

"Well, I've never made a hundred before but I'll willing to give it a try. But I might need some help."

"I's can help!" Clem piped up.

"I'm sure you can. Let's go, then."

Clem ran back into the room and up to Vivi's bed, repeating the entire conversation word for word and ending with a rushed request for permission to go with Sally. Vivi looked toward Cam, who stood with his shoulder pressed into the door frame. He nodded his head, mouthing that Clem would be fine, and Vivi gave her consent. Clem ran out of the room again and Vivi heard her peppering Sally with questions as they moved down the hallway. Vivi fought the urge to call her back. Sally was a stranger. How could she let Clem go off with someone she hadn't vetted?

"Clem will be fine, Viv."

How did Cam know that she was worried? Had her expression said all that? If so, she really had to get her face under control. She could not allow Cam to discern how ridiculously attracted she was to him.

Vivi pulled her gaze off his tall frame, his messy hair. He was dressed in cargo shorts and a sleeveless shirt showing off his broad shoulders, big biceps and his smooth, golden skin. An overnight scruff covered his jaw and he wore flip-flops on his surprisingly elegant feet. She wanted to take a big bite out of him and then soothe the pain away with a long lick.

Vivi dropped her head back onto the pillow and placed her forearm against her eyes. Oh, God, she was in so much trouble.

Vivi felt the bed shift and inhaled Cam's fresh-from-the-shower scent, the heat from his body sliding over her. She felt his thigh against her hip and then his fingers gently pulled her arm from her face. Vivi reluctantly opened her eyes.

"Hello," Cam said, humor in his ridiculously pretty eyes.

Vivi felt her nipples puckering against her T-shirt—his T-shirt—and she licked her lips, noticing there was no moisture left in her mouth. He was too close, and this setting—a beautifully decorated bedroom containing a huge bed—was too intimate. She needed distance to regain some control. She couldn't, wouldn't let Camden affect her like this again.

Then Cam's mouth touched hers and she knew it was too late. He did affect her, in every way. Her lips opened to his tongue, her back arched so that her nipple could find his hand and her legs fell open. She was putty in his hands, a morning mess of melted glue.

Unable to help herself, Vivi linked her arms around his neck, sighing as his thumb brushed her nipple, smiling when he yanked her shirt from under her butt so that his hand could find her skin. He brushed her hip, stopped when he realized that she wasn't wearing any panties and then carried on, his fingers skimming over her stomach and rib cage. As his tongue swirled around hers, sipping and sucking and rediscovering her, his hand found her breasts, giving both his attention.

Vivi allowed her hands to roam, exploring the hard muscles of his back, the width of those impressive shoulders, the taut muscles in his arms. He was so powerful, utterly and fundamentally masculine. Ignoring her aching body, Vivi wiggled closer, needing to have every inch of her body plastered against his.

Preferably naked and preferably immediately.

Cam wound his arm around her waist to haul her in and Vivi couldn't help the whimper of pain when his hand connected with a bruise on her back. Cam cursed and immediately lowered her to the bed. When he pulled back, Vivi saw the concern in his eyes and knew that the spell was broken.

Dammit.

Cam tugged her forward, pulled her shirt up her back and knelt on the bed to look over her shoulder. His mouth thinned and his eyes cooled; he looked thoroughly, utterly pissed off. Why?

Feeling self-conscious, Vivi pulled the shirt under her butt and the covers up to her waist. She pushed a hand through her messy hair and looked at a point past Cam's shoulder. They shouldn't be making out. That was part of their past, and it couldn't be part of her future. There couldn't, shouldn't be anything more between them but Clem, but desire—hot, fast and insistent—kept popping up and making its irritating presence known.

"You have a bruise the size of a dinner plate on your lower back and another on your shoulder blade,"

Cam said, his voice laced with frustration. That was when she realized that he wasn't pissed off at her but for her. He wasn't happy that she was hurt. And his obvious concern ignited a small fire in her stomach. When had anyone last cared how she was, how she felt? God, she couldn't remember. When she was a young teenager? A child? Maybe not even then. She was her mother's showpiece, her pet, her sense of self-worth. The one object Margaret Donner had control over.

"Any other bruises?"

Vivi thought about brushing his question off but quickly realized that if she didn't give Cam an answer that satisfied him—i.e. the truth—he'd pull up her shirt and find out for himself. Any other man would get a black eye if they were to be so bold. Cam, on the other hand, might just get lucky. Dammit.

Vivi pursed her lips before replying. "Top of my right thigh and on my knee."

Cam pulled back the covers and pushed up her shirt, whistling when he saw the livid purple and black bruises. His fingers brushed over her injuries, his touch too light to cause any pain, and his eyes met hers. "Sorry, honey."

Vivi shrugged. "I'm a bit stiff and a lot sore but I'll live."

Cam brushed his thumb over her cheekbone before his fingers picked up a loose curl and tucked it behind her ear. The gesture was so sweet and tender, so at odds with his big hands and hard-ass attitude, that Vivi felt the sting of tears. Tenderness was such a foreign emotion.

"I'll bring up some pancakes and a dose of pain-killers," Cam told her, his tone telling her that he'd not entertain any arguments. "Then you can get some more sleep."

"I need to be with Clem."

Cam looked past her to the window, his expression tight and guarded. When he met her eyes again, his held a range of emotions she couldn't identify. "I know we haven't spent enough time together for you to trust me, Vivi, but I wish you would. Please believe that I would never, ever let anything happen to Clem. I might only know her for a day but she's my daughter, my responsibility."

"Cam, I don't trust easily." Or at all. And she never, ever let anyone take control. Of her or her daughter.

"I'm asking you to trust me for a few hours. We'll stay in the house. And if we do go outside, we'll keep in shouting distance of the house. I just want to give you a chance to rest, to heal." His mouth quirked up into a smile that she found hard to resist. "And I'd like to get to know my daughter."

She was tired and sore, and she'd love to go back to sleep. Could she release the reins for a couple of hours and allow Cam this time? Vivi stared down at her clenched hands, taking some time to think. By making Cam her emergency contact person she'd created this situation. Cam was now part of Clem's life. She'd have to let them spend time together at some point, and if she wanted Cam to be a good father to Clem, that meant allowing them to spend time together alone. At some point she'd have to trust Cam. Why couldn't she start now? An experienced child-sitter was in the house if Cam ran into difficulties with Clem, and Vivi would be just a shout away. What could go wrong?

Nothing except that Clem might fall in love with Cam and she might fall in lust with Cam—oops, too late on that one—and the whole situation could blow up in her face.

God, she was so damn tired and so damn sore. She just wanted a few hours…

"Okay. Except that I will take the painkillers and skip the pancakes."

Vivi saw the relief in Cam's eyes and underneath, the determination. "Nope, you'll put a hole in your stomach if you take the meds like that. Pancakes, coffee and a full glass of water and then you can have the drugs."

He stood up and Vivi tipped her head up to scowl at him. "Did anyone ever tell you that you are as bossy as hell?"

Cam smiled down at her and her stomach flipped over once and then, because it could, did it again. "All the time." He dropped his head and brushed his lips across hers in a slow, gentle, supremely sexy kiss. When he lifted his mouth, he smiled at her. "Then again, like recognizes like, sweetheart."

* * *

Not so far away, Angela Perry heard the front door to her apartment opening and started a mental countdown.

Four.

Three.

Two.

One.

"You kissed Ryder Currin? In the hallway? At work?"

Angela lowered the bottle of water she'd been guzzling and arched her eyebrows at her best friend who'd just made liberal use of her just-for-emergencies key. Tatiana Havery was perfectly made up and immaculately dressed for eight thirty on a Saturday morning. Angela, makeup free and perspiring from a five-mile run, felt grubby and gross. "I'm going to shower. Can we discuss this later?"

Tatiana wrinkled her nose and waved her hand at her damp clothing. "Your shower can wait until we are done discussing the ludicrous rumor I'm hearing about you kissing the very hot Ryder Currin!"

The word "kiss" was too tame a word for what had happened yesterday. Inhaled? Devoured? Scarfed? Any might work but she certainly had not simply *kissed* Ryder.

"Why do you assume it's a rumor?" Angela asked, a little pissed because Tee made it sound like Ryder was so out of her league. "I did kiss him and it was amazing."

Tatiana's mouth fell open. "You did not!"

Angela couldn't help her small smirk. "I so did." The smirk morphed into a self-satisfied grin. "And it was freakin' amazing."

Tatiana lifted her eyebrows. "I can see that it was. Lucky you." Then a second later, "Or unlucky you."

Angela frowned at her friend. "And what do you mean by that?"

"Part of the job of being your best friend, honey, is keeping your feet firmly on the ground. So I'm reminding you that the man you just locked lips with allegedly had an affair with your mom. And there's also a chance that he blackmailed your grandfather into giving him land."

Tee's caustic statement blew away her warm and fuzzies. Dammit, she'd forgotten. How could she? But Ryder had told her that there was nothing more between her mom and him than friendship, and she believed him.

Didn't she?

"He explained that they were just friends."

"But you can't be sure, can you?"

She couldn't, dammit. She only had the word of a man she'd been taught not to trust.

"You know what your dad always says, Ange. Trust but verify."

"And who can I ask about the past who doesn't, to quote Dad again, have skin in the game?"

Tatiana considered her question. "Why don't you go back up to the ranch, find someone who has worked on the ranch, in the house, for a long time and ask what they remember? Servants know everything and someone will know if anything happened between your mom and Ryder."

It wasn't a bad suggestion, but Angela wondered whether it was worth the effort. "The thing is, Tee, I really do believe Ryder. While we haven't had much time to discuss the details, my gut tells me that he's telling the truth about the past."

But what if she was wrong? What if she simply wanted to believe Ryder? Was her desire for him confusing the issue?

"What should I do, Tee?"

Tatiana waited a beat before responding. "Like I said, go to the ranch and ask some hard questions. Because if something does develop between you and Ryder, you'll will always have this cloud of doubt hanging over you. Rather get it sorted now before you are in too deep."

It was sound advice, even if it was delivered in Tee's normal shoot-from-the-hip manner. Unfortunately, it was advice Angela really didn't want to hear. Or take.

Much later that Saturday, when Cam finally heard footsteps in the hall, it took all his willpower not to bound to his feet like a lovestruck puppy. It didn't matter that his heart was suddenly revving in the red zone or that his mouth was as dry as the Mojave Desert. He was a grown man—he should know better. Cam kept his eyes on the screen of his laptop and waited until he heard Vivi clear her throat before he slowly raised his head to look at her.

And instantly felt the sharp punch to his heart.

With her makeup-free face and hair pulled back, she looked like the young woman he'd seduced all those years ago. He'd sent Sally out to purchase some clothes for Vivi and Clem, and the denim shorts she'd bought made Vivi's legs look endless. The T-shirt boldly proclaiming "We the people like to party" skimmed her high breasts and her subtle curves. She was sunshine after a brutal storm, hot chocolate after shoveling snow, a breath of fresh air in an empty house.

She was both lightning and soft rain, strength and fragility, more beautiful than he remembered and more terrifying than he could've imagined.

God, he was in so much trouble. "Neck-deep, bleeding and swimming with alligators" kind of trouble.

Vivi pushed her hands into her back pockets and rocked on her bare feet. Sexy bare feet tipped with pale pink nails. "Hi. Where's Clem?"

It took Cam a moment to understand her question. Clem? Right, her—his, their—daughter. "Uh, we gave her a sandwich and some juice, and she fell asleep while watching *Peppa Pig*. She's in the media room, two doors down."

Vivi frowned and stepped into his office and up to his desk, allowing her fingers to trail over the edge of his antique walnut desk. "I don't let her have a lot of TV time…for future reference."

"You don't?" Cam asked, surprised. "Why not?"

"I prefer for her to do puzzles or to look through a picture book. Too much TV numbs the brain," Vivi replied, sounding defensive.

Cam saw her mental retreat and silently cursed. "That wasn't criticism, Vivi, just a need to understand." He glanced down at the screen, wondering how to frame his next sentence, wondering if he should even verbalize his thoughts. But they needed to be said, and he needed to say them. "I spent the morning with Clem and she's…"

He should never have hesitated because it gave Vivi the chance to clench her fists and for fire to jump into her eyes. "Be careful what you say next, McNeal. I don't give a damn what you think about me, but don't you dare criticize my daughter."

Cam frowned, appalled that she would instinctively assume that he was about to pass judgment on her. He slowly stood up and folded his arms, wondering who had made this strong, vibrant woman assume that she'd be the victim of harsh criticism.

"I was going to say that I think Clem is a bright, happy child with a sharp mind and an extensive vocabulary. She's funny and interesting and sweet."

He would've been amused at her shocked expression if he hadn't been so angry on her behalf. Why did she expect reproof instead of praise? Why did she immediately brace herself for bad news?

"Judging by that amazing human tornado asleep on my couch, you must be an incredible mother," Cam said, holding her gaze and hoping she'd see that he meant every damn word. And more.

Vivi searched his face for any hint that he was lying, and when she finally seemed to accept that he wasn't, her shoulders fell and her cheeks flushed. He thought he saw a hint of tears in her brown eyes but she lowered her head too quickly. When she replied, her voice was husky with emotion.

"Thank you. But she makes it easy. She really is an incredible child." Vivi took a little time to lift her head, and when she did, her expression was inscrutable.

"I need you to know that I spent a lot of time thinking about how to tell you about her. About *whether* to tell you about her," she finally said.

A part of him wanted to be angry at her, to rail at her for denying him Clem's first months and years, but another part of him, a bigger part, wanted to understand her hesitation.

"I did some research on you and everything I read led me to believe that you wouldn't be interested in being tied down, in having a child."

Really, that was her excuse? She was a terrible liar. "You are old enough to know that you shouldn't believe everything that is written in the press, Vivianne."

Vivi wrinkled her nose and drew patterns on the Persian carpet with her toes.

"Why did you really not want me to know about Clem?"

Vivi looked him in the eye and shrugged. "I didn't want you to think that I wanted your money. We do fine on our own."

Now that wasn't a lie, but it wasn't the complete truth, either. But he'd take the little she was prepared to give him. For now.

"Talking about money," Vivi said, looking ill at ease again, "I hate to do this but I need to get to the DMV on Monday to get a new license so I can get hold of some money. When I do that, Clem and I will find somewhere else to stay."

This again. He had a massive house, plenty of space and ample money. He could support two dozen families and consider it petty cash. He'd had many girlfriends who'd seen him as nothing more than a pretty face, a nice body and a healthy bank account. Yet Vivi wanted to prove, at every turn, how independent she was.

It shouldn't turn him on but it did. Hell, everything about her did—from her walk to her talk to her mouth and legs and voice and stubbornness and bravery.

"So, would that be possible? Or, if that's not something you want to do, could I get a loan to get there by cab?"

She made it sound like she was asking him to invest millions in a fly-by-night start-up instead of a loan of under a hundred dollars. "I'll drive you on Monday."

Then Vivi smiled at him and his heart ballooned and his pants tightened. Yeah, as he'd said before, he was neck-deep in trouble, all right. And was that an alligator snacking on his ass?

Seven

Vivi burst into tears when she walked through the doors of The Rollin' Smoke. The main seating area was still covered in an inch of water, but judging by the dark stains on the walls, the floodwater had swamped the leather-covered benches within the booths and knocked over chairs and tables. Her eyes immediately examined the rare photographs of long-ago Texas that hung on the walls, and she was relieved to see that most looked undamaged. The chairs and tables and the flooring could be replaced but the photographs couldn't.

Clem, who sat on Vivi's hip, patted her cheek. "No cry, Mommy."

Vivi felt Cam's broad hand on her back and

turned her head to look up at him. "Yeah, don't cry, Mommy. It's all fixable."

Vivi bit her lower lip. "It's such a mess, Cam."

Cam's hand drew big circles on her back. "It's just stuff, Viv. Nobody got hurt, that's the main thing."

Vivi hauled in a deep breath, grateful for his succinct and pointed assessment of the situation. He was right—it was just stuff, and everybody who worked here was okay. It was, as he said, all fixable.

"Joe! Joe!"

Clem's piping, excited voice made Vivi turn. She saw Joe, her boss, friend and mentor, standing in the doorway to her kitchen, looking ten years older than before. This restaurant was his life's work, his baby. And his employees were his family. For him, this was like losing his home.

Vivi picked her way through the debris and walked straight into his arms, sighing when his big, brawny arms encircled her and her child. This man was her family, her sounding board, more than her own father had been. Vivi buried her face in his shirt and let the tears fall. She felt Joe taking Clem into his arms, and then his hand was rubbing her back and she felt his lips in her hair. "Shh, baby girl, it'll be okay."

After a few minutes Vivi raised her face and reached for the kitchen towel Joe always kept tucked into the waistband of his pants. She wiped her eyes, sniffed and sent a worried-looking Clem a shaky smile. "It's okay, baby, Mommy is just upset that the horrible flood made such a mess."

Clem pursed her lips. "So, no mac-cheese today?"

Vivi smiled and Joe laughed. Clem always ate Joe's specially-made-for-her pasta dish when she visited the restaurant.

Vivi looked around at the damage and forced the question from between clenched teeth. "So, how long are we going to be out of business?"

Joe ignored her to greet Cam, whom he'd met before. Vivi saw the speculation in his eyes, knew that he was wondering what was happening between Cam and her. She'd be getting a phone call later and demands for an explanation.

Joe led the way into the kitchen and placed Clem on the stainless-steel counter. Vivi smiled when Cam came to stand next to the table, one hand anchoring her small thigh so that she wouldn't tumble to the wet floor. He was already a protective dad. God help Clem when she was sixteen and wanting to date. Vivi boosted herself up onto the counter to sit next to her.

"Are you okay?" Joe demanded, cupping her face in his big hands, his eyes skimming her face. "You said that you had an accident and that you were fine, but I know you, Vivi. You treat an in inch-deep cut as a scratch."

Cam opened his mouth to speak and Vivi tossed him a don't-you-dare scowl. Joe didn't need to know how close she'd come to death; he had enough to deal with as it was. "I'm fine, Joe. I just have a couple of bruises." Wanting to change the subject, she looked around. "Where is everybody? I expected the staff to be here, cleaning up."

"It's Sunday and I sent them home," Joe said. "They are exhausted, and many needed to spend time at their own homes."

Vivi gripped the edge of the counter and asked again, "When do you think we can open?"

Devastation flashed in Joe's eye and Vivi's heart plummeted into free fall. When Joe dropped his gaze from hers, ice-cold panic skittered through her veins. "Joe, what's wrong? What's the matter?"

Joe placed his hands behind his head, sent Cam an uncertain look and lifted his shoulders in a small shrug. "I don't know if I can ever open again, Vivianne."

Jesus! What?

"Why?" Vivi demanded, the word almost sticking in her throat.

"I'm underinsured. Grossly underinsured," Joe admitted, pain and remorse coating every word. "I have some savings but I don't think I have enough to cover the cost of another renovation."

Vivi lifted her fist to her mouth. "God, Joe, no."

Joe took her hand. "I know how much you need a job, Viv. But I've been making some calls and I already have positions lined up for you, at some of the best restaurants in the city." He managed a small smile. "Some are even at better wages than what I offer you."

"But I don't want to work somewhere else. I want to work with you," Vivi said, disconsolate.

"I was going to pass this on to you, hand over the reins in a year or two, give you some shares." He kicked a plastic bottle floating at his feet. "Now I can give you nothing. I am so sorry."

Vivi saw the disgust on his face, the shame, and hopped off the counter to take his hands in hers. She waited for Joe to look at her. "Joe, you have already given me so much. You gave me a job when I was down to my last two dollars, without money to feed my baby or to buy diapers. You arranged for Charlie to look after Clem while I worked, and you looked after her when she couldn't. You taught me to cook, you gave me a way to support myself and my child. You gave me everything!" Vivi squeezed his hands. "Don't you dare apologize, not to me, not ever." She shook her head, determination coursing over her. "And I refuse to work for anyone else. We are going to resurrect this place."

Joe shook his head. "There's not enough money, Vivianne."

There was always a plan to be made, money to be found. Vivi had learned that years ago. When she was at her lowest, when she thought that she'd have to reach out to her mom for money to feed Clem, things had worked out right. The universe had yet to let her down and it wouldn't this time, either. She would find a way to reopen The Rollin' Smoke. It might not be as big, or employ as many people, but she'd reopen it, dammit. She just had to get creative and find a way.

"I'll do it, Joe. We'll do it," Vivi told him, her throat closing when she saw the relief in the older man's eyes. He wasn't alone and neither was she; they'd do it together.

They were a team, dammit.

Cam had wanted Vivi from the moment he saw her walking into that dingy bar in Tarrin, all long limbs and curly hair and wide, deep brown eyes. The sex between them had been explosive, and if he'd stuck around he would've been tempted to see her again.

Three years ago he'd sensed that she was still part girl, slightly naive and innocent, but she'd told him that she was up for a one-nighter and he'd taken her at her word. But that girl was a pale version of the woman Vivi had become. As a mother, friend, employee, she was dedicated and loyal and determined. And he wanted her with an intensity that threatened to knock him off his feet.

She was flippin' amazing.

But as much as he admired her, he was also a realist.

After putting Clem into her car seat and buckling her in, Cam climbed into the driver's seat and turned to look at Vivi as he started his car. "That was a hell of a promise you made Joe," he said, keeping his voice mild. He knew how much it cost to set up a restaurant, having invested in one over a year ago, and he doubted Vivi had any idea of the reality of the promise she'd made.

Vivi met his gaze and lifted finely arched eyebrows. "You don't think I can do it?"

Careful, McNeal, you are wandering into a minefield. "I'm coming to believe that you can do anything you set your mind to."

"But?"

"Putting Joe's place back on its feet will be a mammoth undertaking. It'll require guts and drive and determination." And money. So much money.

"You don't think I have those traits?" Vivi asked, her voice so devoid of emotion that he suspected he'd just detonated a mine. And that the explosion could only be heard in her head.

He was still trying to choose his words when she poked his arm with her index finger. He pulled his eyes off the road and caught the fury darkening her gaze and the annoyance thinning her lips. He could handle her anger, but the disappointment in her expression—at him—slew him.

Before he could speak, Vivi's low-pitched voice drifted over to him. "You have no idea what I can and can't do, McNeal. Yeah, you might have built this empire in three years but you didn't have to do it while you were pregnant or with a baby on your hip. I left home with a hundred dollars in my pocket, scared out of my head. I had no job prospects, no skills and no one to call since my mother banished me from my family and my town. Since all my friends were part of her church, I lost them, too. I slept in shelters, and one memorable night, on the streets. Do you have any idea how terrifying it is to know you have a child who's totally and utterly dependent on you for everything and to not know where you're going to sleep that night, how you're going to feed her or clothe her?"

Vivi pointed at the restaurant, her finger shaking. "That man in there gave me a chance and then a dozen more. He taught me to cook, to create. He was my salvation and my warm place to fall. He took me in when my mother and the world spit me out. I will part seas and move mountains for him—and I will rebuild The Rollin' Smoke—because he gave me a chance when no one else would."

The fierceness in her voice was a tangible force, as was the intensity in her expression. He felt like their combined effect was pressing against his chest, pushing him back into the seat. Not often at a loss for words, Cam opened his mouth to speak and closed it again, unsure where to start. He was pretty certain that Vivi hadn't meant to open the door revealing her past, but now that she had, he'd take the opportunity to look inside. He had so many questions.

"Your mom banished you?"

Vivi hauled in some air and closed her eyes. When they opened again and met his, he saw a mixture of emotions flash through them—determination and sadness tinged with anger. "Yeah. She insisted that

I have an abortion, that my being unwed and pregnant would be a scandal she'd never recover from and that it would diminish her standing in her church."

Wait...what? That didn't make sense. "Aren't churches supposed to be against abortion?"

Vivi's smile held no amusement. "Apparently, it's an acceptable option when your position as the highest-ranking female, the moral authority, is threatened. She made it very clear that I either leave or have an abortion."

"Did you call her out on her hypocrisy?"

Vivi shrugged. "Even if I had bothered to argue, nothing I said would've changed her mind. Besides, I'd been thinking of leaving for a while. Pregnancy forced me into action."

"Why the hell didn't you get in touch with me?" Cam demanded.

Vivi sent him a "get real" look. "I told you. I didn't have your surname or your cell number. And you'd told me you were leaving town but you didn't tell me where you were going. I didn't have the first clue how to get hold of you. I thought that you were a one-off encounter, so you can imagine my shock when I saw you at Joe's."

"I still don't understand why you didn't make contact then, why you chose not to tell me about Clem." Most women would've been all over him like a rash, demanding, at the very least, substantial child support. Even Emma now found him socially acceptable. She'd contacted him shortly after her divorce, wanting to reignite what they'd once had.

Money, it seemed, made a lot of wrongs right.

Vivi turned around, took a long look at Clem, who was half dozing in her car seat, and handed him a cool, pointed look. "I can give Clem everything she needs, Cam."

Sure, maybe she could. She could feed her and clothe her and send her to school. But she couldn't give Clem the one thing he'd needed the most growing up. "But you couldn't give her a father, Vivianne. So answer this—if you didn't nearly die yesterday, would you ever have reached out to me? Told me about her?"

Vivi's silence was all the answer he needed. Cam looked away, annoyed and confused. He was angry, sure, but he also thought that, maybe, her instinct to keep Clem from him was right. What type of father was he going to be? He was a driven workaholic, someone determined to show the world that a Mc-Neal could be successful, that a McNeal could hold on to a dollar for longer than a millisecond, that a McNeal could build a business, keep a job. He didn't know how to be a parent, to think about someone else, to put a child first. He'd spent most of his life looking after himself. He had no reference point, having come from a long line of messed-up, childish, irresponsible men.

Feeling sad, annoyed and totally at sea, Cam accelerated away. He had a child, he was a father and he was also totally in lust with Clem's mother. So where to go from here?

Back to River Oaks, he supposed, not that he would find any of the answers he needed there. It was just a house, not a home.

Vivi made it to Tuesday night without ripping Cam's clothes off and doing him against the nearest wall—which was not an easy feat. Also equally heroically, she managed not to put a pillow over his face when he was sleeping. Alternating between lust and annoyance, she felt like she was not only living her life in someone's else's house but also on a knife-edge. She was mentally exhausted; all she wanted was a break. From feeling horny and from insisting that Cam keep his credit card in his wallet.

"You cannot buy me a car, McNeal."

Cam, recently returned from dropping Clem off at Charlie's, looked up from buttering his toast and grinned. "How do you plan on stopping me, Donner?"

Semantics. "You can obviously buy me a car. I just don't want you to," Vivi responded, trying to hold on to her patience. "My insurance money should be in soon and if transporting Clem is a problem—"

"Which it's not."

Vivi ignored his interruption. "—I can take a taxi. But the point is, you cannot buy me a car." She pushed away the brochures he'd handed to her, knowing that if she looked at his suggestions, she might have a harder time saying no.

"No. A thousand times no. You cannot spend money on me."

"Why not? " Cam slapped jam on his toast, took a bite and chewed, his eyes dancing. He wasn't taking her seriously, dammit! "It's just money. I'm paying to have Clem's room turned into a nursery and you worked with the interior designer on Clem's room."

"Worked with" was overstating her involvement in the process. Yesterday, after visiting the DMV and her bank, she'd watched as a crew of men delivered a rocking chair, a bed and a chest of drawers to the room opposite the master bedroom, the one two doors down from her own. The interior designer— some bright-eyed blonde Vivi was convinced had shared sheet time with Cam—asked her whether Clem was a pink or neutral baby. Vivi told her that her daughter liked bright colors, but Clem's room was now a masterpiece in beige and cream. Clem didn't like her new room, which was why she still shared Vivi's big bed. Vivi was okay with that—if Clem slept with her, there was less chance of her inviting Cam to do the same.

"Clem doesn't seem to be particularly enthralled with her new room," Cam commented.

It's rich but it's as boring as hell. As dull as dishwater. But Cam was proud of what he'd done for Clem, so she couldn't hurt his feelings. "She's only two, Cam. And she likes the books."

There were lots of books in her new room, and

Vivi was grateful to have new material to read to Clem at night.

"You could've saved yourself a fortune if you'd just spoken to me instead of going through your bland interior designer, but—"

Cam placed his piece of toast on his plate. "Bland? She decorated every room in this house."

"And it's beautiful," Vivi quickly responded. It was utterly gorgeous, but…

"But…? I can hear your *but*."

Vivi winced and decided that he was a big boy, he could handle the truth. "But it has absolutely no personality. There's nothing of you in this house."

Vivi thought she heard Cam murmur "exactly," but that didn't make any sense. Why wouldn't he want to live in a house that reflected who and what he was? His house should be filled with bold colors, interesting pieces of art, tactile accessories. Cam McNeal was anything but bland.

But how Cam decorated his house had nothing to do with her. She wasn't staying. In a few days—the authorities were asking residents to stay away for another week but Vivi was convinced they were being overly dramatic—she'd be back at her house, among her things, things that reflected her personality.

"The point is—"

Cam lifted a "hang on" finger when his phone rang. He picked up the device and after a couple of "yups" and a "that's fine" and a "look after yourself," placed the phone back on the table. "Sally isn't coming in today. She has a bad case of flu and she feels awful."

Oh…

Oh!

That meant that she and Cam were alone in the house. Wanting to keep Clem's routine as normal as possible she'd sent her to day care and, as a result there was no Clem to interrupt them or Sally to consider. Totally, utterly alone. Vivi knew the moment Cam realized the same thing, because his eyes deepened and focused on her mouth. His blatantly hungry stare sent a river of lust down her spine, pooling heat between her legs. She knew that if she moved, gave him the smallest sign of encouragement, they both could be naked and screaming in a heartbeat.

She really wanted to get naked. She might not scream but she'd definitely moan.

"Camden."

It was one word, small but potent, and he heard her unspoken demand. *Come over here and kiss me.*

Cam released a low growl and Vivi watched, fascinated, as he rocketed to his feet, the fast movement causing his kitchen chair to topple over. By the time the chair hit the floor, she was in his arms and his mouth was on hers, his tongue sliding past her teeth to take possession of her mouth. He tasted like strawberry jam and coffee, sweet and hot, and those sparks he mentioned morphed into a dozen fireballs.

Wanting to get closer, Vivi pushed her breasts into his hard chest, curling into his heat. She wanted more, needed to see him, taste him, have access to those gorgeous muscles. Vivi lifted her hands and attacked the buttons on his shirt, silently cursing when the buttons refused to cooperate. Cam solved that problem by pushing his hands between them, the backs of his hands scraping over her nipples. He gripped the sides of his shirt and ripped it apart. Buttons scattered and Vivi quickly pushed his shirt off his shoulders, down his arms. She needed to feel his skin, his heat. Standing on her toes, she pushed her mouth against his, wanting a harder kiss, and Cam obliged.

He tilted her head by holding the back of her head while his other hand pulled her T-shirt up her back, allowing cool air to touch her back. He was only her second lover, and this was only the third time she was doing this, but she didn't feel self-conscious or shy. How could she when Cam interrupted his kisses with compliments, telling her how hot she was, what he intended to do to her? She was inexperienced but that didn't matter. Cam was in control.

Right now, in this instance, she let him be.

Vivi muttered her displeasure when he pulled his mouth off hers so that he could do away with her shirt, but a second later his hands covered her breasts, his thumbs teasing her nipples and his mouth trailing down the side of her neck.

Cam kissed her, finding all those long-neglected places craving his touch and a few that she didn't know existed before this moment. She was fire and heat and need and want, a pulsing field of energy that started and began with him. If she wasn't so desperate for this to end in a big bang, Vivi would've been worried about how precisely in tune with each other they were.

They were ice and cream, milk and honey, matches and gas-soaked kindling. They *worked*, somehow bigger and better than before.

Vivi sucked in a breath as Cam pulled her nipple into his mouth, sucking her through her bra. Frustrated by the barrier, she reached behind her to unhook her bra and pulled the fabric down her arms, her breath catching at Cam's now blue-black eyes.

If the massive erection tenting his cargo shorts wasn't a clue, then his dark eyes would've been. He wanted her. Right here and right now. And having such a man—strong, virile, so experienced—desire her made her feel powerful and intensely feminine.

As Cam bent his knees to suck her nipple, Vivi locked her arms around his head, dropping kisses onto his wavy hair. She sighed as his teeth scraped her and whimpered when he moved his mouth across her breast to her sternum and licked his way down to her stomach. Cam hit his knees and his hands gripped her hips, his thumbs on her mound. Vivi couldn't help herself, she rotated her hips, silently telling him what she needed. Cam used one hand to flip open the button to her cotton shorts, and when the fabric fell to the floor, he gently inserted his finger into the V of her panties and ran his finger down her thin strip of hair.

"Is this what you want, Vivi?"

Vivi shook her head and couldn't get the words past her tongue. When she didn't answer, Cam sat back on his heels and stared up at her, his finger flirting on the edge of her clit. "Vivi, I need to know… can I carry on? *Should* I carry on?"

Vivi nodded and pressed his hand into her, lifting her hips so that he had better access to her secret places. She released a small cry of pleasure when his finger stroked her, skating over her folds and slipping into her wet channel.

"So wet. So hot," Cam murmured.

Vivi widened her legs and wrapped her arms around her waist, assaulted by the waves of pleasure. God, she was teetering on the edge of an orgasm. But she wanted him inside her, filling her, completing her.

"Come inside me, Cam. I need you."

"Protection."

Vivi shook her head. "I'm on the pill."

Cam surged to his feet, one hand fumbling at the band of his shorts. Vivi swatted his hand away and slipped the button from its hole, gently sliding his zipper down. Reaching under the band of his underwear, she freed him, wrapping her hand around his thick, pulsing cock. Vivi looked down and sucked in her breath. Like every other part of him, it was so beautiful, ferociously masculine.

Cam's compliments dried up and it was his turn to whimper. She stared down at him, her fist encircling him, her thumb sliding across his tip. Wanting to feel every part of him, she spread her fingers out so that she cupped his balls, gently massaging him. Cam jumped in her hand and she felt his shudder. Yeah, control wasn't anything either of them possessed anymore.

This time, this one time, control was severely overrated.

Vivi gasped when Cam wrapped an arm around her butt and lifted her up and into him, walking her to the breakfast table. She heard the crash of plates, the ping of cutlery hitting the tiled floor, and then she felt the cool wood beneath her back, her legs being pulled apart. Cam stood between her knees, his eyes glittering, his cheeks flushed. He removed her panties and then he was probing her entrance, thick and hard and wonderful. Vivi dug her heels into his hips and pulled him forward and Cam sank in an inch. He closed his eyes and she watched, fascinated as he fought for control, fought the urge to plunder and pound.

But she wanted both. Using her core muscles, she did a sit-up and wrapped her arms around his neck, pulling him down so that his mouth met hers.

Against his lips, sucking in his sweet breath, she murmured the words: "I need you. Now."

Cam's thumb skated over her cheekbone, across her lower lip, and he left his thumb there when his mouth enveloped hers. As his tongue slid inside her mouth, his erection pushed into her and she felt sensations she'd never felt before.

Overwhelmed. Taken. Fulfilled. Completed.

Vivi was on the verge of shattering when Cam's mouth turned tender. His kisses became more thoughtful and he slowed his hip action, taking her down an inch. Vivi murmured in protest and tried to insert a hand between their bodies but Cam pulled her hand away to place it on the table next to her hip. Pushing his hand under her butt, he lifted and tilted her and Vivi felt him scrape an area deep inside her. She didn't want to come, not yet, but she couldn't stop her free fall...

Exquisite sensation battered her and she willingly stepped into the ball of energy, allowing Cam to sweep her away. As she tumbled through space, through galaxies both familiar and undiscovered, she was vaguely aware of Cam's shout, his tense body, him pumping his seed into her. Then he joined her to dance on the stars.

Back on earth, her eyes flew open and she stared up into Cam's shocked face. "What the hell was that?" she muttered.

"God knows," Cam responded, his hands on her hips. Vivi dug a fork out from under her butt and tossed it to the floor. She stretched back against the table, arched her back and then realized that Cam, still inside her, was, astoundingly, still hard. She could've sworn that he'd come, too.

Cam pushed a strand of hair off her forehead and smiled softly. "I came, I saw, I was blinded in the process. But something about you, apparently, makes me recover superfast."

Vivi's eyes widened. "Uh, I, we…holy…" Cam covered her breasts with his big hands and played with her nipples and Vivi closed her eyes, loving the sensation. "That feels amazing."

Cam sank himself a little deeper and Vivi felt herself melting…straining for more. Cam smiled, dipped his finger between their linked bodies and found her clit, rubbing his thumb over her most sensitive spot.

Vivi climbed. And climbed. And within minutes, she was ready to fall apart again. Apparently he wasn't the only one who recovered fast.

Eight

Vivi stood in Joe's ruined kitchen, looking at the list of everything they'd lost in the fire. She lifted her head when she heard the front door open and the sound of masculine footsteps headed in her direction. Looking down at her grubby white T-shirt and filthy jeans, she hoped the representative from the insurance company wasn't an hour early—she'd hoped to clean up and change before meeting with him.

Vivi laid her clipboard on the steel table and raked her hair back from her face, securing her heavy ponytail with a band from her wrist. Picking through what was left of The Rollin' Smoke was hot, dirty and sweaty work and she was glad she'd sent Joe home to rest. Her old friend was not taking the loss of his restaurant well and whatever pain she could spare him, she would.

Vivi bit her lower lip, wishing she hadn't been so reckless with her promise to resurrect this place. After spending a few days among the detritus, she was starting to think that rebuilding Rollin' would be impossible. The insurance payout would barely cover the replacement costs of a third of the equipment they needed and none of the furniture. They was no provision for loss of trade and they had just enough money in the company account to pay the staff this month. It was clear that they'd have to release the staff and tell them to find new employment.

She had savings and job offers in her in-box, but she knew that most of her colleagues lived from paycheck to paycheck. Unlike her, they weren't living in a mansion with a billionaire who was determined to make up for years of not paying child support. She'd lost the battle on the new car—she was now, temporarily as she told him, driving a nifty new Jeep—and Cam had hired a personal shopper to restock their closets as her house was still off-limits.

There hadn't been any argument about her moving into his bed. Being with him, loving him and having him love her, was exactly where she wanted to be. She could handle playing house for another week or so. She'd enjoy his spectacular body, the fast, expensive car and living like a princess for the next week, and then she'd go back to real life.

"Hey."

Vivi saw Cam in the doorway of the kitchen and returned his smile. And man, he had a hell of a smile. It made her feel all gooey inside, like a perfectly cooked chocolate brownie. Vivi closed her eyes and shook her head. She was losing it, comparing Cam's smile to a brownie, his body to a work of art, his eyes to the color of the Mediterranean Sea...

"Enough, dammit."

"Sorry?"

Vivi did a mental eye roll. Now she was talking to herself? Cam McNeal should come with a danger warning.

"Nothing, ignore me." Vivi tipped her head to receive his kiss, a gesture that was becoming as natural to her as breathing. Which was a bad thing since she was leaving his daily life in a short time. "Hi."

"Hi back." Cam's thumb brushed against her cheek and he lifted one eyebrow. "You are a hot mess, Vivi."

At least he'd qualified the mess with *hot*. "I know. I've been trying to ascertain if anything in here can be salvaged."

Cam kept his hand on her back as he looked around the damaged kitchen. "And can you?"

Vivi shook her head. "Very little. The smoker, the industrial ovens and the electrical equipment were all soaked and the electrics fried. And even if they could be rewired, they are now a health risk. The crockery and cutlery have been washed and boxed but that's not worth a whole lot. The furniture in the restaurant all needs to be replaced and the entire building needs to be repainted. It's going to add up to tens of thousands of dollars, Cam."

Cam picked up her clipboard and flipped through her papers. When he grimaced, Vivi's stomach sank to her toes. "Basically, you're looking at setting up a new restaurant, Viv."

She nodded. "I know."

"Can Joe take out a loan, approach his bank?"

Vivi wrinkled her nose and placed her elbows on the table, holding her face in her hands. "I'd like him to, but he's close to retirement age, Cam. I'm asking him to take out a huge loan to rebuild a restaurant when it makes better sense for him to take the insurance money and invest it."

It was hard facing the truth but Vivi had experience in dealing with the reality of the situation, not the fantasy. Okay, she was living a fantasy life with Cam in his lovely house in the best area in town, but that would end. Real life wasn't housekeepers and fancy cars, a hot man in her bed, a full-time dad for Clem. Her future reality would be dropping Clem off with him for weekends, having him around for Clem's birthday parties, discussing their daughter's progress on the phone.

She could look at the future and see it clearly… and Rollin' didn't have much of a chance. In fact, if she gave Joe permission to retire—she knew he was only sticking around because of her—it would cease to exist. It was looking increasingly likely that she'd have to find a new job, in a new kitchen, run by people who neither knew her nor cared about her. She wouldn't be able to bring Clem to work, to take time off when she needed to, and wouldn't have the freedom of being her own boss.

"I think this is it, Cam."

Vivi felt his big arms surround her, felt the kiss he placed in her hair before he bent his head to place his cheek against her temple. "We'll find a way, Viv. Let me help."

She wanted to allow him to pick up her clipboard and wave a magic wand, throw some money at the problem and restore Rollin' to what it was. He was rich enough to do that, astute enough to make it work. But if he did that, if she allowed him to take over, it would just be another thing she lost control over, another part of her life that she'd have to share with Cam. Rollin', her job here and the people were *hers*. She'd washed every dish, learned every recipe, developed her own. She'd nagged and moaned and laughed with her staff, mentored them as Joe had mentored her. This kitchen was her domain, the one place she had complete hold over. If Cam became involved, because he wasn't the type to sit on the sidelines, she'd lose autonomy.

She might as well go and work for another restaurant.

"I can help you, Vivianne. Let me," Cam whispered in her ear.

But then it wouldn't be hers. It would be his because Vivi knew that he who held the cash exerted the control. She shook her head and patted the arm that was hooked around her waist. "Thank you but… no. Everything comes to an end, and this, I think, is the end of this journey."

She felt Cam stiffen and he jerked away from her. She slowly turned and saw the disappointment on his face and, worse, the hurt in his eyes. "Why won't you let me help you? I invest in companies, in case you've forgotten, and I'd like to invest in you."

If she wasn't sleeping with him, if she wasn't the mother of his child, would he still be making the same offer? If she came to him as a stranger, would he be jumping in as eagerly as he was now? She didn't think so. "It won't work, Cam."

"Why the hell not?"

Vivi folded her arms and made herself meet his eyes. "Because then it wouldn't be mine. It would be yours."

His sexy mouth thinned. "I don't understand."

"If you threw a vast amount of money into this place, you would then become my boss, and this wouldn't be my happy space anymore. While I don't own any shares in this business, Joe treated me like a partner, not an employee."

"And you don't think I can do that?" Cam demanded, irritation coating his words.

"I think you like your own way and you are not scared to demand it," Vivi said, carefully choosing her words.

"I have many interests in many businesses. I can be a silent partner."

"Could you be that with me?" Vivi demanded.

"I don't see why not." His frown deepened at the skepticism he saw on her face. "What? I can back off."

Yeah, sure. "Like how you backed down when I said I didn't need a new car? The way you listened to me when I told you I didn't need a personal shopper, or that Clem was too young for a professionally designed nursery? It's like you hear my words but they have no meaning."

"That's because you are stubborn!"

"No, it's because you are controlling." Vivi whipped back. She waved her hand around, trying to encompass the kitchen. "This has been my domain for three years. I know every inch, every piece of equipment. I know that the mixing machine sticks on three, that the oven is a half degree off, which pan makes the best sauce. This is my domain, Cam."

"And I'm trying to restore it to you!" Cam yelled, obviously frustrated. His anger didn't frighten her, so Vivi didn't react when his words bounced off the walls. "I want to give you what you want, what you need!"

And wasn't that the problem? She didn't need him to ride to her rescue. She could save herself. She'd done so three years ago, made something of herself without his help, and she could do it again. She *needed* to do it again. She couldn't allow herself to rely on him, to let him become her safety net, because she understood that people were fallible and frequently let you down at crucial moments, mostly when you needed them the most. No, it was better to rely on herself, only herself.

And if that meant giving up Rollin', then she would do exactly that. She'd just find a new spot, make a new home.

"You are stupidly, ridiculously, irrationally independent!" Cam stated.

"I worked damn hard for it, Cam. I won't give it up."

"But how much are you prepared to sacrifice in your bid to remain independent? Where's your red line?"

She didn't know.

Before she could answer him, not that she had an answer, Cam shook his head, obviously disappointed. "I'll see you at home, Viv."

Home, Viv thought, her thoughts immediately going to the house in River Oaks. Dammit, it might be his home but it wasn't hers. She was confusing fantasy with reality again.

She was not a lead character in a rom-com movie and Cam was not her happily-ever-after. Real life was hard, gritty, messy. It was best that she remembered that before life slapped her sideways again.

Ryder had thoroughly enjoyed this evening and the company of his friend Camden and Camden's new woman, Vivi, who cooked like a dream. He looked at the younger man who sat in the chair across from him, his daughter lying in his lap. Cam reminded him of his younger self, reckless, brave, so very convinced of his firm grip on life. Only now did Ryder realize how little he'd known then.

And after sharing a quiet family dinner with Cam, his brand-new daughter and the woman who was currently turning Cam's life upside down, Ryder realized how much he missed having a family, being part of one.

Yeah, his first marriage hadn't worked out, but he'd adored Elinah, his second wife, and she'd loved him back. He remembered many nights when Maya had fallen asleep in his arms, her sweet face tucked into his neck.

Looking at Camden's daughter, he recalled how fifteen years ago, Maya—the child of his heart but not his genes—had often been curled up like that, her mouth pursed. Now she was eighteen and demanding he tell her the exact details of her birth, about how she arrived at their house under circumstances that most people would term as suspicious. A tiny girl with medical issues...

How did he even start to explain? What words would he use to unravel the tangle that was Maya's birth? Hell, even Maya's biological mother didn't know that he was raising the daughter she'd given up nearly two decades ago. And he had no intention of her ever finding out that Maya was, originally and for a very brief period, hers.

Maya was his, and Elinah's. Why couldn't that be enough for his headstrong daughter?

Pushing those thoughts away, he glanced at Clementine again. God, he missed that, missed the time when his kids were young. Carrying them up to their rooms, then carrying Elinah to their bed.

Camden was—impatiently, he was sure—waiting for him to leave. Because Ryder knew it would annoy him, he accepted Vivi's offer of a second cup of coffee. His mouth twitched at his friend's scowl.

"Is the TCC meeting still on for tomorrow?" Cam asked.

Ryder nodded. "Yep."

"Then I'll see you there," Cam hinted. Ryder smiled and ignored his not-so-subtle jerk of his head in the direction of the door.

Cam scowled at him again before releasing a resigned sigh. "You never told me how your meeting with Sterling Perry went last week, Ry. Did you challenge him to pistols at dawn? Or swords at sunset?"

Cam loved taking the piss out of him. He was one of the very few people he'd allowed to do that. "Sterling wasn't available."

But Angela Perry had been...

Ryder shifted in his chair. Holy hell, he was fifty years old and it had been a long time since he'd been that turned on. Oh, he'd had several affairs since Elinah died—he wasn't a damned monk!—but those had always been about getting his rocks off. Kissing Angela had been…awesome. He'd have been happy to stand there and kiss her for another five, ten, fifty minutes. Since that kiss, his brain felt fried, and all he could think about was the way she stepped up and into him, laying those cool, pink lips on his. Her long, lean body with its subtle curves pressed into him made his head swim.

Dammit, he was utterly and completely attracted to Angela Perry—the daughter of his rival. What the hell was he going to do about it?

Cam noticed Ryder's expression change and wondered at the hint of panic he saw on his old friend's face. The bastard should've left a half hour ago and Cam knew, by the laughter dancing in his eyes, that he was hanging around purely to piss him off. But now the laughter was gone and worry turned his eyes a deeper shade of blue.

"Thank you, darlin'," Ryder said, taking a glass of whiskey from Vivi, who resumed her place in the corner of the overstuffed leather sofa.

Vivi asked Ryder about his kids and Cam looked down at his child. Clem, dressed in pale purple pj's with spotted dogs printed on them, was sprawled across his lap, legs and arms spread wide. Her eyelashes rested against her cheek, her perfect, rosebud mouth pursed. In sleep she looked like a porcelain doll, picture perfect. In real life, she was a walking, talking Energizer Bunny. The kid never, ever, stopped. Cam was an active guy, fit and strong, but Clem wore him out. Okay, she and her mother wore him out. The hours after Clem went to sleep were his and Vivi's and they didn't get to sleep until the wee hours of the morning.

It was as if they both realized that their time together was limited, that they had to take every moment given and enjoy every second. They were both acting like this couldn't last, like they were living on borrowed time.

Cam looked down at Clem and reminded himself that he'd soon run out of excuses to keep Vivi and his daughter with him. At some point, they'd return to their cottage in Briarhills and he would be left alone in this house. He looked around at his informal, tastefully decorated living room and realized that the only thing giving the space warmth was Vivi's presence.

Cam tuned out of their conversation, thinking about the way Vivi made him feel. He just had to look at her and his heart rate accelerated, his mouth dried up. He'd had lovers before but none, not even Emma, had made him feel so off balance. Sex had always been another basic function, something he enjoyed and forgot about. But sex with Vivi was different, wild and intoxicating. He couldn't get enough of her.

Whatever was between them was different from anything he'd ever experienced and he had no clue how to handle it. Before Vivi and Clem, he'd been content to live his life alone, but now he didn't know how he'd go back to that solitary life when they moved out.

He couldn't define what he and Vivi had but it wasn't meaningless. And he wasn't enthusiastic about rambling around this mausoleum on his own. He liked hearing Clem's high-pitched laughter, her tiny footsteps, her piping voice and her off-key singing. He liked coming home and seeing Vivi in his kitchen, sharing a glass of wine with her at the end of the day, watching her bathe their daughter. He wanted her to stick around and teach him how to be a dad, to let him share her bed and her body, have her explore his.

He liked this life with them in it.

But could he have it? Did he deserve it? He was, he reluctantly admitted, a controlling bastard. He liked calling the shots; of course, he did. He'd been a child without guidance, too much freedom and not enough discipline. He had run wild and free, with no sense of responsibility and no concept of accountability. Eventually he'd taken a path away from crime, but a part of him always thought that no matter how much money he made and how much he gave away to charity—anonymously, of course—he was stained by his past actions.

His daughter was pure goodness and Vivi was pure class. How could he possibly think he was good enough to be with them on even a semipermanent basis?

It would be so easy to lie to himself. To tell himself that he had a right to happiness, that he wasn't the same person. But he knew he was, deep inside. He'd translated his ability of reading people to scanning the business world with an eagle eye, looking for an opportunity to pounce. He was still the same person—hard, driven, wily and cunning. Except now he just operated in a field that was legal. He was still the boy with a chip on his shoulder, constantly wanting and needing more. He'd never been satisfied with much for long, always looking for something new, something he'd never had.

What if, in time, Vivi and Clem weren't enough, what if he wanted more? What then?

Cam was jerked out of his thoughts by Vivi's hand on his shoulder. He looked up into her lovely face and his heart bounced off his chest.

"I'll take Clem up to bed."

He nodded and Vivi scooped Clem up, easily holding her in her arms. Cam glanced at his watch, saw that it was getting late and asked if she was going to come back down.

Vivi shook her head. "You spend some time with Ryder." She turned to smile at the guest. "It was so nice to meet you, Ryder."

Ryder and Cam stood up, and Ryder's smile was easy. "I look forward to eating at your restaurant again soon, Vivi. I miss your ribs."

"That's kind of you to say." Vivi's smile held sadness and Cam reminded himself that he had to do something to convince her to allow him to bankroll the restaurant's resurrection. He'd find a way past her independence and stubbornness. Her dream deserved that.

"Please tell me that's she's going back to work," Ryder said once Vivi had left the room.

Ryder was so damn sharp, immediately picking up that something was off about Vivi's response. He trusted Ryder and told him the truth. "Joe was underinsured and wants to retire. Vivi isn't able to raise the cash needed to reopen."

Ryder sat down and placed his ankle on his knee, his whiskey glass nearly empty. He shook his head when Cam offered him more. "So, get a group of investors together and fund the renovation," Ryder said, frowning. "You've it done a hundred times before."

Like he hadn't considered that idea a thousand times. "She's won't let me. I've never come across anyone more independent or stubborn than Vivi Donner."

Ryder chuckled. "She doesn't want your money?"

"Neither my money nor my help," Cam admitted.

"That's hilarious."

It really wasn't. Cam poured himself another whiskey and frowned at his friend's amusement. "I want to give her what she needs but she won't take a damn thing," he grumbled.

Ryder dropped his foot, leaned forward and handed Cam a hard look. "Are you sure that money is what she most needs from you?"

Cam met his eyes. "Probably not, but I can't give her anything else, Ryder. She needs a good man, a man with no baggage, someone who isn't…me."

"Camden," Ryder sighed his name. "Please tell me this isn't about that horse crap Emma spouted so long ago."

Emma had just verbalized what Cam knew to be the truth. "I can't be the husband and father they need. I'm not—" He hesitated, unable to voice his deepest fear. He wasn't good enough for them.

"Jesus, Cam." Ryder pushed his hand through his thick hair. "Dammit, boy, when are you going to knock that chip off your shoulder? You're not that kid you were, the person you were. People can change, Camden."

"I'm terrified that I'll let them down, Ry."

"That's part of being a dad, Camden, part of love. We all feel like that at one time or another. I felt like that with all my kids, and doubly so when Maya came along."

Cam cocked his head, interested. "I thought you would've felt more confident by then, having had Xander and Annabel already."

"I worried that I couldn't love Maya the same way I loved the kids of my blood, that I'd let her down, that I'd fail her."

"You adore Maya," Cam pointed out.

"Of course, I do. I love her with every fiber of my being," Ryder retorted. "She might not carry my DNA but she's my kid, every gorgeous inch of her."

Cam wondered whether he should ask and then shrugged. What the hell, Ryder would or wouldn't answer. "How did you come to adopt Maya? How did she come into your and Elinah's life?"

Ryder stared at him before looking away. A few seconds later, he spoke again.

"So what I'm trying to tell you is that every father has doubts, we are all scared. And anyone who isn't doesn't have the brains to realize how hard the job is," Ryder said, obviously choosing not to answer his question. Fair enough. It was Ryder's business after all.

Ryder stood up and placed his glass on the coffee table in front of him. Cam followed him to his feet and tried not to squirm when Ryder stared at him. "If you gave yourself the slightest chance, the smallest break, you'd realize that you'd be a great dad, Cam. Despite your past, you're as honest as the day is long, and your streak of integrity is a mile wide. You are not the boy you used to be. You'll be fine."

Cam released some tension and wished he could embrace Ryder's words, to trust himself as Ryder seemed to trust him. But he'd have to start doing that, if he was going to be the dad Clem needed him to be.

"You'd also make a really good husband." Ryder grinned at him. "Bad boys always do."

Ha-ha, funny.

Not.

Nine

Cam looked a little lost and very alone when he walked into his bedroom later that night. From the window where she stood, way on the other side of the room, Vivi watched him sit on the edge of his huge bed, his elbows on his knees, his fingers tunneled into his hair. His shoulders, usually so broad, were hunched and he stared at the hardwood floor beneath his feet as if it held all the secrets to the universe.

She'd suspected that he wouldn't come to her tonight, wouldn't make the first move for them to spend the night together. So, after putting Clem in her bed and showering, she'd slipped into Cam's room to wait for him. He'd been perfectly charming during dinner tonight, but as she laughed with Ryder and heard stories of Cam's past, she'd felt him retreat. His eyes had deepened, held more shadows, and he hadn't engaged in the conversation. Vivi knew he was mentally walking away from her and she wondered why.

"Hi."

Great opening line, Donner. Surely you can do better.

Vivi watched as Cam slowly turned around, his expression inscrutable. He tried to hide his feelings but his dark, beautiful eyes told her that he wanted her. It was in the way his gaze lingered on her legs, on her chest and her mouth before his eyes slammed into hers.

"You want me," Vivi stated, her voice stronger.

"You're a beautiful woman. I'd have to be dead not to," Cam replied, lifting his feet onto the bed and placing his hands behind his head. The big muscles in his arms bulged and she had to grip the drape to keep her feet in place. Because if she didn't anchor herself to something she'd be stretched out over him and reaching for that bulging zipper.

Concentrate, Vivi. "But you don't want to want me. You don't want the possibility of us."

For an instant Vivi thought he might deny her statement, but at the last minute he snapped his mouth closed and schooled his features, deliberately placing his hand over his erection. "It's late, Viv. Are we going to do it, or can I go to sleep?"

Vivi blew out her breath as she struggled to hold on to her temper. He was being a jerk and she wasn't going to let him get away with it. She told him as much.

His eyes widened at her statement and his hand fell from his groin to rest on the comforter next to him. Knowing that she couldn't allow him the opportunity to talk or walk away, she moved quickly and talked faster. "Let's talk about what's freaking you out, McNeal."

When he stayed silent, Vivi crawled onto the bed next to him, crossed her legs and placed her forearms on her knees. "My being here, Clem being here, is starting to feel less like playacting and more like real life, huh?"

His nonanswer was an answer in itself.

"Sometimes I feel like you want us to stay, other times I feel like you can't wait for us to leave."

Cam's fingers tapped the cotton comforter. "I enjoy spending time with Clem."

"But you're not enjoying me?"

Cam lifted his eyes and she saw his confusion. She understood it. So much had happened in such a short time that it was hard for him to wrap his head around it. But they had to, because this wasn't just about them. They had a daughter to consider. If Vivi was confused about what was happening between her and Cam, then Clem—bright as a button and an absolute barometer when it came to reading emotions—would start feeling confused, too.

"I love—" Cam hesitated and Vivi knew that he was picking his words carefully. He didn't want to hurt her but knew that he would anyway. "—this. The sex, it's awesome, Vivi."

It *was* awesome. "But?"

"But I can't be what you want, what you need."

Oh, this was going to be interesting. "What do you think I need, Camden?"

"I think you need and deserve it all, Vivianne." Cam lifted one big shoulder and let it drop. "I think you deserve the big house and the nifty car and not having to worry about cash ever again."

Whoa, hold on a second...

Before Vivi could tell him what he could do with his house and car, Cam spoke again. "You deserve a partner, Viv, someone who will be with you to celebrate the big and the small, to hold you when you are sad and pick you up when you are down. You deserve someone who will stand beside you, someone who thinks that your happiness is more important than anything else." Cam hauled in a deep breath. "I'm not that person, Viv."

She wasn't so sure. "What makes you say that?"

Cam shot to his feet and jammed his hands into the pockets of his casual pants. By the way the fabric bunched, she could see that his hands were clenched into tight fists.

"I'm a selfish bastard, Vivi. I was raised to be like that. My father and grandfather were the same. My entire life has been a fight for survival, to get ahead. I don't think about other people. It's all about me."

What rubbish. A selfish person didn't offer his money to help her rescue a failing restaurant, didn't run to the bedside of a stranger when he found out he was an emergency contact, didn't lavish time and attention on the daughter he'd just discovered was his own. No, how Cam saw himself wasn't who he was.

"I see I've shocked you. Well, while I'm at it, let me get this done." Cam's voice was pitched low but Vivi saw his distress in his rigid neck, his thin lips, his taut shoulder blades. "I was a childhood thief, Viv. I could lift anything, anywhere, anytime. I could steal your watch or your purse and you wouldn't even know it. My father and grandfather were equally proficient in the art of pickpocketing, grifting, conning. Crime, you see, was so much easier than a day's work."

Now was not the time to speak, so Vivi just looked at him, refusing to show any of the shock she felt. If she did, she'd lose him.

"I grew bored with petty crime— Oh, that's the other thing. I get bored really, really easily."

There was a subtext there and she was bright enough to decode his sentence. *I'll get bored of you. I always do.* She could challenge that statement, but it wasn't time yet. Frustration passed over Cam's face, probably because she wasn't throwing up her hands and squealing like an offended teenager. She was stronger, smarter, than that.

Instead, Vivi just lifted her eyebrows in a silent "Is that all you've got?"

"I graduated to breaking into people's houses, even stealing into bedrooms while couples slept. You see, I'm not a good bet," he said, suddenly looking tired and defeated, washed out and embarrassed. "I've had a tough past and I'm a tough bastard and I doubt I'm going to be a good father…but I'm going to try." He shook his head. "But I can't be more than that, Vivianne."

She didn't respond to his last statement. Instead, she focused on his past. "Tell me, Cam. Tell me all of it."

Cam took a deep breath before shrugging. "It's not pretty."

"I don't want pretty. I want the truth."

"My mom left when I was two or three. My father said she couldn't handle it, couldn't handle me."

Even if his mother had been that much of a bitch, how dare his father repeat her words? Vivi pushed her fist into her sternum, immediately and intensely angry for the child Cam had been.

"Most people expect our parents to love us more than anything else in the whole world. I never did. I knew my mom left because she didn't love me and I knew I was nothing more than a burden to my father. When my grandfather came to live with us when I was five or so, he reinforced that idea. I was a drain on their resources, and if I was going to hang around, then I was going to earn my keep.

"I remember being five or six, and them teaching me to pick pockets, boosting me through small windows to pilfer items out of bedrooms and offices. Even then I knew what we were doing was wrong, but they told me that if I did this one thing, they would throw a ball with me, read me a story, buy me an ice cream. It was all about bribery, and they were masters at knowing exactly what I needed most at that time. They were damn good at manipulation."

Vivi wanted to throw something, to punch a wall, to go out and find his relatives so that she could strip skin off them. "Where are they now?" she asked, holding on to her temper.

"My dad is in jail, and will be for the next twenty years, and my grandfather died a few years back."

"Ah."

"Have you ever met a person who was never, ever at fault?" Now that the plug had been pulled from the dam, the river of words started to flow from Cam.

From his expression, Vivi suspected that it might be the first time he'd spoken about this, so she nodded, encouraging him to talk.

"They were always victims, you know? They always blamed someone else, frequently me, when something went wrong. They were Teflon coated. They never took ownership or responsibility for anything, ever. And they didn't teach me to do that, either.

"I spent my life analyzing my behavior, trying to be the person they wanted me to be. I was perpetually tired, drained, partially because I was constantly worried they'd be caught and I'd be shoved into the system. Turned out I was the one to be arrested first, and I was the one tossed into the system."

"You went to jail?"

Cam nodded. "Yeah. You've been sleeping with an ex-con, sweetheart."

"No, I slept with *you*," she was quick to correct him. "Why did you go to jail? And what happened inside that made you straighten out?"

"I went to juvie for burglary. My lookout, my father, ran when a silent alarm went off in a house. I got caught red-handed with my hand in a safe."

Vivi grimaced. How scared he must've been.

"And I was straightened out by a social worker who arranged for me to tour a prison, someplace I realized I didn't want to go. She told me that if I didn't shape up, some of those animals I met would be my new best friends." Cam shrugged. "I've never been stupid, so I shaped up. By the time I left juvie, Dad was incarcerated and I decided not to contact my grandfather again."

"That must've been hard."

When Cam shook his head, it finally hit Vivi how hard his life must've been. How alone he must've felt. "I'm sorry, Cam."

"I'm not a good bet, Vivi." Cam looked her in the eye. "I was exposed to stuff that no child should be exposed to. I did things no one is supposed to. My father and his father had screaming fights and frequently came to blows, so I never learned how to communicate in a healthy way. Can you understand why I'm so damn reluctant to settle down, have a family?"

"But you do have a family. You have Clem. And me."

"And I don't deserve either."

He uttered that sentence with such conviction that it tore into Vivi's heart. How could he still believe that? He'd come out of a dreadful situation to become an amazing man, a great human being. It was easy to be successful when you had the benefits of a supportive family and a good education. He'd had none of that, yet he'd been determined to better himself. She was crazy about him—possibly in love with him—but she also admired the hell out of him. And respected him more than that.

"I can't fix my past, Viv."

"Nobody is asking you to do that." Vivi rested her hands on his chest. "But you can focus on the positive aspects of your past, the fact that you changed your life around, that you had the guts to do that. Give Clem the love and support you missed. Break the McNeal cycle."

"I don't know if I can."

Of course, he could, Vivi wanted to tell him. He already had. Why couldn't he see that? He was tough, bold, wonderful. She didn't understand how he could look at himself and see a failure. But didn't she do the same? Didn't she refuse all offers of help, reject anything that threatened her independence because she was still living in the past? Because she was still allowing her mother to control her actions?

So, wow. Light-bulb moment.

But this wasn't about her right now. This was about Camden. She could sit here and tell him he was being unbelievably hard on himself, that she pretty much thought the sun rose and set with him, that she wanted to see where this went. But she knew that nothing she said would make him change his mind.

But maybe she could show him.

Yeah, sometimes actions spoke so much louder than words.

Vivi stood up and walked over to her badass billionaire and rested her hands on his hips, her forehead on his chest. She felt the tension seep from him, just a little, and she traced the hard ridges of his stomach. Nuzzling her nose into the gap between his first and second button, she inhaled his spicy, masculine Cam smell. Wanting more, she pulled his shirt from the waistband of his pants and placed her hands on his hot skin, up over his ribs, his nipples and up to his powerful shoulders.

Needing more, she tugged his shirt up and over his head, sighing her pleasure when she had unrestricted access to his chest, his back, his stomach. After licking his flat, dusky nipple until it formed a tiny peak, she tracked her mouth over his shoulder and dipped her tongue into the deep groove between his muscled shoulder blades, then traced her lips over a scar on his back. She smiled when his hands came up to touch her thighs.

"I thought we were fighting," Cam said, his voice low and rough.

Vivi wrapped her hands around his erection, hard beneath the fabric of his chinos.

"You were trying to pick a fight with me, but I wouldn't let you," Vivi told him, keeping her voice soft. "You're not ready to believe anything I have to say. So I thought I'd try something different." Vivi dropped kisses on his spine, bending her knees to kiss the hollow of his back, just above the waistband of his pants held up by a thin leather belt.

She frowned and tugged at the offending object. "Crocodile, McNeal? Uh, no."

"What's wrong with the belt?" Cam demanded and she finally, finally, heard a note of amusement in his voice.

"It's a reptile! Ick." Vivi ducked around him and took off the belt. She dragged her thumb up his hard erection and smiled at his quiet shudder. After attacking the button, she pulled the zipper down and looked into Cam's beautiful, confused face. Good. Confusion was better than his relentless quest for control.

"You are so very beautiful, Camden McNeal."

Cam blushed, leaving Vivi to wonder if anyone had bothered to compliment him before. She cupped his face in her hands and stood on her tiptoes. "Your body is magnificent, your face is too sexy for words, but, man—" she tapped her fingers against his temple "this brain of yours slays me."

Vivi dropped back down to her toes and kissed his chest, somewhere in the region of his heart. "And your heart is as big as the Texas sky. You just don't want anyone to know that."

"Vivi," Cam pleaded, "*don't.*"

Vivi shook her head. "Don't what? Tell you I want you, tell you that I'm not only attracted to your body but to the awesome person you are?"

Confusion was evident on his face. He opened his mouth, but no words came out.

Vivi smiled at him. "All you need to do right now is kiss me, Cam. Can you do that?"

Her quiet question seemed to jolt Cam out of his shock. His hands gripped her hips and he was lifting her up and onto him. Vivi wrapped her legs around his hips as his mouth took hers in a kiss that was a perfect mix of amazement and confusion, desire and tenderness. She sensed him trying to keep his passion under control, but when she sucked his tongue into her mouth, he utterly and finally lost control.

Oh, not of his strength or of the moment but of his need to hide, to run, retreat. It might not last but Vivi knew the exact moment that he surrendered to whatever this craziness was between them, fully embracing their madness.

Suddenly his hands were everywhere, kneading her breasts, cupping her butt, skimming her back. His mouth ravaged hers before he traced his tongue down the column of her neck, sucked the sensitive skin inside her collarbone. The buttons on her shirt popped and he lifted her up his chest so that he could tongue her nipple, sucking her lace-covered breast into his mouth.

Vivi cradled his head and sighed, knowing that here, in his arms, she was completely connected with the person he really was. The thought pushed hot liquid to her core and she felt her moisture soak her panties.

She wanted him buried deep inside her. Now. Immediately.

Unable to wait, Vivi whispered a dirty suggestion in his ear and Cam pulled his head back, blue-black eyes glittering.

"No."

Her suggestion had been explicit and, if she had to say so herself, damn hot. He should be tearing her clothes off, not staring at her like she was a tasty ice pop on a scorching day. Well, now, this could be interesting, she thought. She leaned back and rested her hands on his shoulders, confident that he could hold her. There was something so sexy about being held by a strong, hot, almost naked guy. The mere thought caused another mini flood down below. He was going to have to do something about that soon.

"What do you have in mind, McNeal?" she demanded in a haughty tone.

"This, for starters." Cam plumped up her breast and took her nipple into his mouth, his eyes still on hers. God, this was hot. Vivi felt her heart pounding, the beginning of an orgasm starting to build.

She really didn't want to go over the edge on her own. "Cam, seriously, I want to come, and I want you there with me."

Cam lowered her onto the bed and quickly, efficiently, stripped her of her clothing. Then he shucked his pants and underwear, his erection thick and hard.

"Faster or I'm going to handle my problem myself."

Cam had the audacity to grin at her. "Go for it, sweetheart. I'd love to watch you getting yourself off. And then I'll just take you back up again."

Such confidence. And absolute truth. Because he was still standing there, far too far away, Vivi narrowed her eyes at him. She wasn't confident enough to go that far…

And she needed his touch. "You do it so much better. Please, Cam?"

Cam's smile hit his eyes. "Are you begging me, Vivianne?"

"Asking nicely," Vivi countered.

"Sounded like groveling to me," Cam shot back as he dropped to his knees by the edge of the bed. Reaching for her, he draped her legs over his shoulders and slowly licked his way up her thigh.

Vivi squealed and released a curse.

"More dirty words, Donner?" Cam murmured, his breath tickling her feminine folds. "I like it."

"Cam, please," Vivi begged, lifting her hips to bring her core closer to his mouth.

Cam chuckled. "Definitely begging."

Vivi didn't bother to answer, not that she could. Every thought disappeared when Cam kissed her, gently sucking on her clit. She thought she'd reached the pinnacle of pleasure, that she couldn't take any more, and she shuddered, pushing herself against his hot, sexy mouth. But then Cam pushed one finger, then another into her and flicked at a spot deep inside her, and every cell in her body shattered. She shuddered, she screamed, her back arched, her skin flushed.

This was it—the best orgasm she'd ever had. Nothing would ever be as good as this. But Cam proved her wrong yet again when he pushed himself into her, pulling her legs up to accommodate him. He pounded into her, demanding that she come again— that she come with him—and those shattered cells disintegrated again.

Cam tensed, hesitated, and when he sank into her that last time, she felt his shudder and knew that he was there with her, fully in the moment, neither of them in control.

The next morning Vivi ran down the stairs, a broad grin on her face. She felt well rested, a little sore in all those good places that suggested that she'd been well loved—but happier than she'd been in a long, long time. She'd heard that sex was a gateway to the soul, but until earlier with Cam, she'd never experienced it. She'd never understood how powerful sex could be, how making love could open one's eyes and make one shift one's focus. Lying against Cam after the third time they'd made love was the most...*right* she'd ever felt. Vivi felt completely in tune with Cam and was convinced that they were better together than they were apart.

He was what she wanted, the person she and Clem needed. Not for his money or his position, though she deeply admired him pulling himself out of a situation that sounded horrible but because he was strong and protective and loving and flawed. For now, tomorrow, the next ten, twenty, forty, sixty years, she wanted to prove to him how worthy he was of love. He needed to understand that she knew him, that she saw him clearly, that he didn't need to hide who he was or what he'd done.

That no matter how uncomfortable, transparent and vulnerable he felt, she loved him and would continue to love him.

Rich, poor, she didn't care. They were stronger together than they were apart. And she thought Cam was finally starting to understand that. Thank God and all his angels and archangels.

Cam had kissed her goodbye much earlier, told her to sleep in and that he would dress Clem and take her to school. She remembered something about him saying he had a Texas Cattleman's Club meeting later that afternoon and that he might be late.

It was Sally's day off and she had the big house to herself. Thinking that she would take another look at the offers of work she'd received, she walked into the kitchen and headed straight for the coffeepot.

Sitting down at the breakfast table, she stared out over Cam's landscaped garden, enjoying the bright blue sky and the lush vegetation. Pulling the laptop Cam loaned her toward her, she tapped her finger on the cover, unable to flip it open. She really needed to spend some time reading through, and understand-ing, the job offers she'd received. She didn't want to, she wanted to go back to what was familiar, what she knew and loved. Was she being stubborn in refusing to take Cam's offer to help resurrect the restaurant? Was she cutting off her nose to spite her face? Nobody was able to open a new restaurant without investors.

There was being independent and then there was being stupid. Was she being stupid or was she just allowing her new feelings—love and lust and hope and giddiness—to sway her?

She didn't know. But what she did know was that she was in love with Cam, that she probably had been since that night three years ago. He made her temper flare, her heart jump, her libido squeal. He frustrated her and turned her on, made her laugh and made her sigh. He certainly kept her on her toes.

And maybe that was a better reason than her inde-pendent streak to keep her from accepting his offer to fund the renovations. How she was feeling, how she thought *he* was feeling, was a good reason to keep their financial and work interests separate. Why add pressure they didn't need to such a fragile situation?

Everything had its season and maybe The Rollin' Smoke's had passed. And if she let go of her dream of renovating his restaurant, Joe could retire in peace and she could open her own place at some point down the line, when she'd cemented her reputation. Maybe then, she would feel comfortable asking Cam to invest. She'd have more experience, Clem would be older and their relationship would be better able to withstand the rigors of combining business with pleasure.

It was a plan she could live with. But she still needed a job. So Vivi opened the laptop and clicked on the message containing the first proposal.

Ten

Attending the Texas Cattleman's Club meeting was the last thing she wanted to do today but her father was insistent. Annoyed, Angela walked across the massive Perry Holdings boardroom, a room built to intimidate and impose, and glanced at the vast display of refreshments and the full bar. It was more than was needed for a late-afternoon meeting, but Sterling wanted to impress. And as usual, he had.

Ryder would be here, somewhere. They hadn't spoken since their lava-hot kiss last week and she was a nervous cat walking on a hot tin roof. How would he treat her? What would he say?

Too edgy to eat—thank God she rarely saw Ryder Currin or she'd waste away—she saw his dark blond head and, ignoring the swoosh in her stomach, decided to confront the sexy beast. She headed in his general direction, wondering how she could casually insert herself into the conversation he was engaged in. She looked at the man he was talking to and wrinkled her nose. She recognized Cam McNeal but she'd never met him. Oh, well, she'd just have to hold out her hand, smile graciously and welcome them to Perry Holdings. It would all be very civil…

If she could stop thinking about Ryder's big hand on her hip, his sexy mouth covering hers.

"Nice spread," Cam commented, his voice drifting over to her.

Ryder scowled at the food. "Perry always goes overboard."

"Hey, I'm not complaining," Cam replied, reaching for a plate and a small, elegant fish taco. After popping the delectable bite into his mouth, he nudged Ryder with his elbow. "God, Ry, lighten up. You look like you want to set someone on fire."

"Preferably Sterling Perry. Jesus, who does he think he is, calling a meeting of the TCC in his boardroom, in the headquarters of Perry Holdings? And especially given everything else that's happened."

He had to be talking about the discovery of the unidentified murder victim at the construction site. Angela, partially blocked by a screen just behind Ryder, stiffened.

"Look, this is a PR move by Perry, it has to be.

He's just trying to curry favor with the powerful members of the TCC," Cam suggested.

"The *still-under-construction* TCC," Ryder snapped back before continuing. "Or maybe he's trying to distract and evade. Keep our attention on something else while he deals with the fallout of finding that body on his construction site. He might have something to hide."

Okay, she'd heard enough. Angela, her blood now pumping with fury and not with lust—okay, a little lust but she'd ignore it—stepped into their space. They both winced and shame flashed in their eyes. Good. "Don't you think it's rude to malign my father while eating his food?"

Ryder looked like he was about to point out that he hadn't touched anything, but Angela narrowed her eyes at him and he got the message. Cam McNeal cleared his throat and she turned to look at him. He was even better looking up close. Tall (like Ryder), built (like Ryder), rough and ready and so very masculine, he exuded that bad-boy vibe. A woman would need a strong backbone to handle a man like him.

As one needed with Ryder. Right now hers was feeling a little jellylike.

"Ms. Perry, you are completely correct," Cam told her. "I sincerely apologize."

Angela nodded her appreciation and watched Camden walk away. When he disappeared into the crowd, she turned back to Ryder.

"Yeah, apologies," he murmured.

Half-assed, but it was better than nothing. Angela whipped a glass of wine off the tray carried by a waiter. Being this close to Ryder Currin, she either needed wine or a fire extinguisher. God, he was unfairly good looking. She'd always had a weakness for blue-eyed blonds. Because he made her feel off balance and fluttery, she channeled her inner ice goddess.

"May I remind you that Perry Construction has had to do major cleanup at the site due to the flood and we haven't been allowed access to certain parts of the site because it was designated a crime scene? Has everybody forgotten that a man lost his life? That he was shot? We don't know who he is, how he got there…"

"Have the police not asked anyone from your organization to help identify him?"

Angela shuddered. "Apparently his face came into contact with a slab of concrete and crushed his features."

Ryder's intelligent eyes sharpened. "Before or after the flood?"

Oh, he was quick. "They won't say. But if it was before, it would have to be a pretty strong and cold person to pick up and drop a concrete slab on his face."

"Not necessarily. You have forklifts on the site, don't you? It's not rocket science."

Angela grimaced and closed her eyes. Who could do that? And why? Man, people were sick. Her eyes flew open when she felt Ryder's big hand on her arm.

And when he linked her fingers in his and pulled her behind the screen, she didn't protest. She needed his warmth, his strength, just for a moment.

Ryder rubbed her bare skin, from elbow to shoulder. Angela knew that he meant it to be a reassuring gesture but it had the unfortunate side effect of heating her panties. She wanted his mouth on hers, to feel her breast mashed against his hard chest, have his fingers mess up her hair.

"Let me try that again. I apologize if I was insensitive, Angela, and I do respect your views." Ryder sent her a wry smile. "It's no secret that your father and I have a history and that he rubs me wrong. And it annoys me that he won't accept that there was nothing between your mom and me but friendship."

She didn't want to think about any of that, not now. All she wanted was his mouth on hers.

He looked like he wanted the same thing. Ryder dipped his head and she could smell his sweet breath. She lifted her heels to bring her mouth to his a fraction sooner. She genuinely could not wait for his kiss—touching him was that important.

Ryder's lips skimmed hers as a booming voice cut across the room.

"Ladies and gentlemen, if you can take your seats, please."

Ryder pulled back and they exchanged a long look containing enough energy to generate a nuclear power plant. She didn't want to talk about the

Texas Cattleman's Club. She wanted to leave with Ryder and then not talk at all.

Ryder linked his fingers in hers and placed a gentle kiss on her temple. "This isn't over, darlin'."

God, she hoped not.

Across town, Vivi frowned when she heard the strident chime of the front door. She opened the front door to a woman in her midthirties, who looked perfectly cool despite the humid temperatures outside.

"Can I help you?"

The woman gave her a tight smile. She introduced herself and held out her hand. "I'm here about the nanny position."

The...*what?* Vivi shook her head and lifted her hands in confusion. "I'm sorry, what are you talking about?"

"Mr. McNeal contacted my agency first thing this morning and my supervisor set up this appointment. My current family is moving back to England, and as I'm one of the agency's longest and most experienced nannies, they immediately thought of me when Mr. McNeal said that he was looking to interview nannies for his daughter."

Vivi took a moment to process her statement. When the woman started to speak again, she held up her hand for silence. So, shortly after leaving her this morning, after a night of mind-blowing, soul-touching sex, Camden's first impulse was to arrange for a nanny for Clem. What did that mean? What could it mean?

Vivi had no idea, but there was one thing she was sure of: she had no intention of taking Clem away from Charlie, and she most certainly didn't need a nanny. After sending the woman on her way, telling her that there had been a miscommunication, Vivi shut the front door and pulled out her phone. She tapped it against her thigh, debating whether she should call Cam and blast him for making decisions without talking to her first.

But maybe that was what he was expecting her to do and a good reason why she should bide her time and wait and see what else he'd had planned for her day.

Because she was pretty sure there was more to come.

Sterling Perry knew that Ryder Currin was mentally giving him the middle finger and he wished he could walk over to him and put him on his ass. He'd wanted to punch Currin's jaw for years now. Twenty-five years was a long time to keep his hatred under lock and key.

Ten minutes. Ten minutes was all he needed to show Currin who was boss.

Sterling stared down at the hands clutching the edges of the podium, ignoring the thought that his fists were no longer as big, his arms no longer as powerful as they had been a quarter century ago.

But man, how he regretted not taking Ryder behind the barn and whipping the crap into him. Just seeing his insolent face, hearing his name hurtled him back to the past, to when he wasn't Sterling Perry the power broker but Harrington's lackey, the foreman of his ranch. Ryder reminded him of a time when his father-in-law's word was law, when he had no say in anything to do with his future or the ranch. He took orders back then, he didn't give them.

And he'd been the ranch cuckold, as useless as a steer. He'd never had a happy marriage to Tamara— they'd married to consolidate power and wealth— but he'd been proud of his beautiful wife. She was an exquisite woman but they'd never clicked, mentally or physically. He hadn't loved her but he couldn't allow her to be in love with anyone else, either, especially not Ryder Currin, a damned ranch hand. How dare he think he could lay a hand on a Perry, on any piece of his property? He still woke up from nightmares depicting Ryder and his wife rutting, hearing their laughter as they disparaged him. And the fact that Ryder had blackmailed Harrington into handing him land—oil-rich land that had made him a freakin' fortune—still burned like acid in his throat. He couldn't stand it then and he couldn't stand Ryder now. And if the rumors about Currin and Angela seeing each other turned out to be true, God help him…

Sterling heard a throat clear and came back to the present, looking out at the curious eyes trained on

him. Dammit, the room would think he was a dod-
dery old man, something he couldn't afford to happen. Once a thought like that took hold, the members
of the TCC would start thinking that Currin was a
better, younger, more energetic leader and they'd
vote for him as president of the Houston TCC. That
couldn't happen. He was Sterling Perry. Nobody
would run this organization but him.

Sterling released his grip on the podium and
cracked a joke. When he got the required laughs, he
relaxed. These were his people, his tribe. He knew
exactly how to handle them.

"Thank you for giving up your valuable time to
attend this first meeting of the Houston Texas Cattleman's Club."

"Can't be a meeting if there's no board yet, Sterling."

Shut up, Ryder. Sterling forced himself to smile
at Currin's quip but chose not to address the interruption. If he ignored Ryder, maybe others would,
too. "We do have TCC business to discuss, but before that happens, I'd like to take this opportunity
to make a personal statement."

He saw the room come to attention, felt the tension increase. Good, he had them eating out of the
palm of his hand. "I would like to make it clear to
all—" he deliberately moved his eyes to look directly
at Ryder "—potential board members and members
of the soon-to-be-constituted TCC that neither myself nor any member of Perry Construction, or our

holding company, had anything to do with the unfortunate murder at the construction site."

Sterling held up his hand to quiet the room when
murmurs resounded. When he had their full attention
once more, he spoke again. "I have also, with the full
support of my family, decided that Perry Holdings
will bear the cost of restoring the construction site
to its preflood condition. We estimate it will cost a
few million but we'll cover the bill."

His words, when they sank in, raised a roar of ap-
proval and thunderous applause. There was nothing
Texans liked more than not having to put their hands
into their own pockets. Sterling couldn't help his eyes
drifting to Ryder Currin. He immediately noticed that
Ryder's arms were still crossed against his chest. His
expression asked what his lips did not: "What the hell
are you up to?"

The applause lasted for a minute, maybe two, but
Ryder didn't bother to put his hands together. The
rat bastard.

Much later than he anticipated, Cam walked into
his house, looked at his watch and winced. He'd
missed Clem's bath time and she would be fast asleep
by now. Dropping his phone and laptop bag in the
hallway, he pulled down his tie and walked toward
the kitchen, frowning when he saw it was in darkness. Only the small informal sitting room that he
and Vivi usually retreated to after they put Clem to
bed had light.

After only a week they had a routine, a favorite room and spectacular, soul-moving sex. It scared the hell out of him.

Cam swallowed, stared down the hallway and knew he was walking into a minefield. He'd made certain arrangements today and he knew his decisions would have consequences. Those consequences were still to be determined, but he knew, deep in his soul, that he was playing with fire.

Cam stared at the artwork on the wall opposite him—an expensive piece he didn't particularly like—and remembered the terror he'd felt when he left Vivi asleep in his bed earlier that day. She'd all but told him, through her actions and the way she'd made love to him, that she completely accepted him and that she might be in love with him. He hadn't slept, consumed with the idea of testing that theory. Did she really mean that? Or would she bolt at the first obstacle? His family had never managed to stay the course, had always found a reason to disappoint him, and he wanted to see if Vivi stuck or ran.

He'd expected Vivi's call by 9 a.m., shortly after the first nanny showed up at the front door. By noon—and after what should've been three appointments with three different nannies—there was still radio silence. He'd shrugged, thinking that she would definitely call when the local bank manager arrived, bearing papers already preapproving a massive loan to renovate The Rollin' Smoke. He was providing the guarantee to secure the loan but the loan would be in her name, her responsibility. He had no idea how that meeting had gone because, again, radio silence.

It had taken every ounce of willpower he had to not call her, to see if she was still here, to judge her mood and her reaction.

Would she stick or run? There was only one way to find out.

Cam took a couple of deep breaths and walked down the hallway. He hesitated at the half-open door, conscious of his dry mouth and pounding heart before pushing open the door with his foot. He stood in the doorway and looked around the room. He found Vivi sitting on a chair, her forearms on her thighs, her hands clasped and her head bowed.

He cleared his throat but Vivi didn't look up. Oh, God. She had to have heard him. Was she that upset? But good news, she was still here. That was a start.

He walked into the room and headed for the alcohol at the far end of the room. He dumped whiskey into two glasses, chased back the contents of one and refilled his glass before walking over to where she sat. He placed one glass on the coffee table in front of her and sat down on the sofa closest to her.

"Hi. Clem asleep?"

Vivi's face, when she finally looked at him, was blank and cool. "I presume so."

Cam felt a bolt of fear skitter along his skin. "She's not here? Where is she?"

"Charlie has her," Vivi answered him before picking up her glass and throwing the contents back. It seemed she needed the alcohol as much as he did. Not a good sign.

"Why is Clem staying the night at Charlie's, Viv?"

"She's not. I'm going to pick her up when I leave here tonight. Then we are going home, Cam. To our home, where we belong."

She was running. Why had he expected something different from her? God, he really didn't want her to leave.

"This is the point where you ask why we are going, Cam," Vivi pointed out, sitting back and rolling the glass tumbler between her palms.

Cam rubbed his hand over his face, thinking that Vivi looked far too controlled, far too calm for what he'd expected to be a humdinger of a fight. Had he read her wrong? Had he read too much into what happened last night? Why wasn't she railing at him, demanding to know what the hell he was thinking?

"What the hell were you thinking, Camden?"

Well, the question was right but there was no heat behind her words, no anger or emotion. He'd expected her to react in one of two ways—to leave immediately or to rail on him, tell him that he had no right to do what he'd done, that she wouldn't stand for it and never to do it again. And then she'd stay.

He never expected this quiet, still, intense response. What did it mean? Where was she going with this?

"You know that you had no right to arrange a nanny for Clem, that you had no right to organize a loan for me. You knew I wouldn't stand for any of it, but you did it anyway. I've been wondering why."

Cam slowly sipped his whiskey, desperately hoping that she'd put him out of his misery sometime soon. Mentally urging her to hurry the hell up, he forced himself to remain quiet, to see where she was going with this.

"So, the only conclusion I can come to is that today was a test. Last night something shifted between us and you were forced to face the fact that we have moved beyond being parents and bed buddies. That realization scared the hell out of you."

Well, yeah. Essentially.

"And you thought a reasonable response to that was to test me, my feelings?"

Cam winced when Vivi's voice rose and frustration and hurt leaked through that cool mask.

"I do want you to stay, Vivi." It was all he could say, the only words he could form. *"Please don't bail on me, please don't disappoint me"* were words he wanted to scream but refused to let pass over his lips.

"You have a damn stupid way of showing it, Mc-Neal," Vivi whipped back. "Why did you feel the need to test me?"

If he was less of a man, he could deny her charge, find a decent excuse for his actions. If she was going back to work, she'd need a decent nanny—Charlie was getting on in age and Joe wasn't going to be around to fill in the gaps—and she wanted her own restaurant. But he couldn't lie to her. She deserved the truth.

Before he could answer her, she lifted her hand to stop him from speaking. "Don't bother answering. I've already worked it out."

He was interested to see if she came anywhere near the truth.

"You did to me what your father did to you. You did what you know." Okay, she was getting warm.

"Last night you told me that your father would test you, that he'd demand that you do something and then you'd be rewarded with his love. You never told me if it worked."

No, his father always reneged on his promise. Cam never received what he'd been promised.

"You expected me to disappoint you and then you'd have your excuse to push me away," Vivi said softly. "You set me up, knowing I'd never agree to your terms and that would give you the excuse to put the distance you needed between us. Because basically, you're terrified of being loved and even more scared of being disappointed."

Cam stared at her, utterly blindsided that she saw him so clearly, knew him so well.

"They say that in times of emotional stress we revert back to the child we were and you just showed me how true that is. Earlier I was tempted to tell you to take your controlling nature and shove it. It's my instinct to run at the slightest hint of controlling behavior because my mom controlled everything I did and said. And I so nearly did."

Cam gripped his glass tighter. "So why are you still here?"

Vivi's deep, dark, stunning eyes met his. "Because my love for you is stronger than my need to run from being controlled."

She loved him? *Still? How?*

"You love me?"

"That's pretty much the only reason I'm still here," Vivi said, not sounding happy about it at all.

Vivi leaned sideways and picked up her bag from the floor at her feet. She dug around inside, pulled out her phone and tapped the screen. After a minute, she dropped the phone back into her bag and met his eyes. "I just called for a ride and it will be here in five minutes. Just long enough to explain what's going to happen next."

What was going to happen next? He had no damn idea. He was still wandering through this minefield, blindfolded and confused.

"I love you, Cam, and I think, maybe, that you might love me a little, too. I think you want me, want the family we can be, but you're scared. That's okay, I'm scared, too."

Cam looked at her, hope blazing from his eyes. Maybe she'd stay...

"I'm not staying, Cam. I won't be controlled by anything, not you, not my mother and certainly not by your fear and your past. You've got to decide whether you can trust me, trust that I love you, trust that I'm not going to bail on you and you need to do all that without the need to test me, or my love.

"I need a partner who respects me as much as I respect him. Somebody who loves me without qualification, who can accept my love and love me back."

He couldn't let her leave, not without making some sort of effort to convince her to stay. Yet he knew that she might be asking for something he couldn't give. "I can try, Viv."

Viv tried to smile but didn't manage to pull it off. "This isn't about trying, Cam, I need action. There's no room for negotiation on this deal, McNeal. It's all or nothing."

He was still trying to make sense of her words, trying to wrap his head around the fact that she was leaving, when she dropped a kiss on his temple, her hand drifting across his hair. "You know where to find me, Cam. But make damn sure I am what, *who*, you want."

Eleven

It's late but I'm known for working longer and harder than many. But it's been many minutes since I looked at my monitor and gave any attention to the papers on my desk.

It's far more fun to remember every delicious detail of this afternoon's Texas Cattleman's Club drama. In the battle for control of the TCC, Sterling definitely won that round.

I've only ever allowed people to see what I allow them to, so I doubt anybody picked up how closely I observed the unfolding events. I noticed Ryder Currin's annoyance when he arrived at Perry headquarters, and as usual, Sterling got his back up when Ryder walked in. Two cocks fighting over the prize of the TCC, each *thinking that the other is their greatest threat, completely oblivious that neither of them will win.*

I will.

By the time I am done with them both, everything they value will be destroyed. I will make sure of that. I've killed once. I'm not afraid to do it again.

People will remember that I was at the meeting, but nobody will connect me with the demise of the two powerful families. Because I smile and pour on the charm. I can do that as easily as I can manipulate, scheme, plot and plan. The duality of my personality doesn't worry me. I am what I am and nothing is more important than seeing these two men taken down a peg or two.

Or five hundred.

I held many conversations with many people—all boring—while keeping an eye on Sterling. Because I pay close attention I immediately noticed the curl of his lip when something displeased him. Because I know him, I immediately noticed his stiff back, his clenched fist. I followed his gaze across the room and yeah, there was drama.

Ryder and Angela stood in the far corner, and since their profiles were closer to me, I saw their tense exchange. Because I'm not a complete idiot, I quickly clocked the sexual tension bouncing between them. It was so obvious they want to see each other naked, as soon as possible. I flipped my gaze to Sterling and grinned. He'd also realized that Ryder and Angela weren't having a conversation about the weather.

Sterling, never shy, headed their way to confront this newest threat to the status quo and I couldn't help laughing at the fact that a fox was in Sterling's henhouse and, by God, he was determined to shoot it.

The terrible twos should come with a box of aspirin and a complimentary bottle of wine. A magical unicorn and a constant supply of chocolate wouldn't go amiss, either.

Vivi looked down at Clem, now back in her own bed in their house in Briarhills and wondered if she dared leave the room. Clem looked asleep but the last three times she'd attempted to leave the room, Clem's eyes had popped open and high-pitched screaming had left her mouth.

Vivi was done. Physically, emotionally, mentally. She wanted a break.

Oh, who was she kidding? She wanted Cam. She wanted to hand her blaring daughter off to him and have him calm her down, because Vivi knew that the person Clem really wanted, the adult she missed at the end of the day, was her father. Her baby daughter, unable to articulate her frustration, was missing Cam. Vivi could relate because she was feeling the exact same way.

It had been nearly three days since she walked out of Cam's house. And while she remained convinced she'd done the right thing, she still wanted to fall asleep in his arms, wake up to his kisses, hear his deep voice laughing and talking with her and Clem.

But as much as she wanted to drive her replacement car across town—the very basic sedan she'd rented on her own—she forced herself to stay put. She'd told Cam what she wanted. Now the ball was very much in his court.

Waiting to see if he would play it was killing her.

If he came, it wouldn't be easy. They weren't easy people. He'd try to boss her about, and she'd rebel. They'd fight but if they acknowledged that their pasts had left scars and recognized when they were acting from fear, they'd be okay. They just needed to love and laugh and negotiate their way through the hard times. She'd have to keep reminding herself that a partnership did mean relinquishing some control, and he had to believe that she wouldn't bail on him.

They could be amazing—if Cam decided that a family was what he wanted.

Vivi heard her phone beep and walked into her bedroom. She saw his name on her screen and wondered if her heart would ever stop lurching every time she saw his name. Probably not. Cam was her strong drink, her poison, her kryptonite. God, she wished she didn't love him so much.

She opened his message and read the words he'd typed seconds before.

Hey. I wanted to check on how Clem was. I haven't called her because I didn't know if it would upset her or not.

Vivi typed her reply.

She misses you like crazy. I miss you like crazy. She cried for half an hour and screamed for another fifteen minutes. How the hell do you think she is, we are?

She couldn't send that. If she did, he would rush over here, jumping on the excuse that she needed him, if only to help with Clem. No, that wasn't how she wanted him back. She erased that message, typed in a new response and hit Send.

She's good. We're good.

I'm not.

Vivi stared at his reply, confused. How was she supposed to answer him? Should she tell him he knew what to do? That all he had to do was to love them?

She was desperate to send some reply, anxious to end this stalemate between them. But in the end, even though her heart was breaking, even though it felt like her soul was weeping, she didn't reply.

Because nothing had changed. She wanted it all. She couldn't settle for anything else.

All three of them deserved more.

Sitting in the informal sitting room in his home, Cam stared at his phone, wishing that Vivi would respond, tell him what to do. Oh, he knew what she wanted—a family, him, her and Clem as a unit—but he still couldn't wrap his head around the concept. Neither could he stomach the thought of being away from her and his baby for much longer. God, why was this decision so hard to make? Why was he finding it so hard to act? He'd never been so indecisive.

Cam dropped his head against the back of his couch and idly rubbed the area of his heart. He missed them, more than he'd ever believed he would. His house, never the warmest place in the world, was now silent and cold, and his life was empty. Viv and Clem brought meaning and light and laughter and warmth into his world, yet he was sitting here, allowing his life to be dictated by the past.

Maybe he'd punished himself enough for being born a McNeal. Maybe it was time to let all that crap go and trust Vivi's version, instead of believing his version of his past—the one his father had taught him and Emma had reinforced. Maybe he should—

The insistent peal of the doorbell filled the house and Cam frowned. He sat up and looked at his watch. It was past ten, late for a social call. He rocketed to his feet and hurried to the front door, thinking that maybe, just maybe, Vivi was outside, that she'd come home to insist that they be together. He'd say yes, of course. Being with her and Clem was all he'd ever need.

But that wasn't possible. He knew that Vivi was

her home in Briarhills. She shouldn't be. She should be here, with him.

There's only one person standing in the way of that happening and that's you, dumb ass.

Maybe it was time to stop being a dumb ass.

He made his way down the hall as his visitor leaned on the doorbell. Again he wondered who it was and how soon he could get rid of them.

Cam jerked the door open and frowned at Ryder, who had his finger raised to push the bell again. "Do it and die," Cam warned him.

"Still in a good mood, I see," Ryder said, pushing his way past Cam to enter his house.

"Not a good time, Ryder," Cam told him. He wanted to go to Vivi, to see if he could straighten out this mess.

"It's a very good time to talk some sense into you," Ryder said, ignoring the open door and walking down the hallway to the sitting room.

Cam cursed, closed the front door and followed Ryder into the room. Ryder poured himself a whiskey and pointed the glass in his direction.

"I'm sick of you not answering my calls, ignoring business. It's time to get your head on straight, McNeal, and I'm the man to do it," Ryder said, lowering his brows in what Cam called his angry bison look.

"It's not necessary, Ryder."

Ryder was not in the mood to listen. "I've left three messages for you, a couple of emails, and you haven't replied to one."

He sounded like an irate teenage girl. "I didn't think that your idea to host a Flood Relief Gala as the TCC Houston's first fund-raiser required an immediate response," Cam responded.

Some of the wind left Ryder's puffed-up sails. He stared into his now empty glass and Cam noticed his concerned expression. "I'm worried about you, Camden."

There was a lot of truth behind that statement and Cam felt his throat tighten. Ryder's genuine concern touched him. "I'm fine, Ryder, really."

"You might be fine in an 'I like being alone' way but you are not fine in an 'I'm in love' way," Ryder insisted.

Well, he could be if Ryder would just let him leave.

"I know what it's like to be in love, Cam, and I know how it feels to lose the woman you love. And I am so mad at you because I would've done anything to have more time with Elinah, anything at all! But it's your stubbornness that's standing in the way of your happiness and that just pisses me off."

"How do you know that Viv didn't dump me?"

"Because that woman is so in love with you she can hardly see straight. You're the one who has stomped on the brakes because you are scared of love."

"I know."

"Don't you argue with me!" Ryder retorted, obviously not hearing Cam's reply. "You haven't had a long-term relationship. You never even date the same girl twice! I've never seen you respond to anyone the way you do with Vivi. It's like she's switched on a light inside of you."

Exactly. "I know, Ryder," Cam said, trying to be patient.

"She's your Elinah, Cam. Why can't you see that and do something about it instead of hanging out in this god-awful house and moping?"

Okay, his house was quiet and a little cold but "god-awful" was pushing it. He needed to get Ryder to listen.

"Well, I'd really like to remedy that, Ryder, but instead I'm standing in my sitting room with an old man who seems intent on lecturing me about getting my head out of my ass. Just in case you're having a hard time keeping up, given your age and all that, I'd really like to go and win my woman back. So if you wouldn't mind leaving…?"

Ryder frowned, grinned as the words sank in, and frowned again. He picked up his dark brown Stetson, jammed it on his head and folded his arms. "Who are you calling old, boy?"

"You," Cam replied, unperturbed. He placed a hand on Ryder's back and pushed him in the direction of the front door. "And you called my house god-awful."

"It is," Ryder insisted, stepping into the hallway. "But maybe Vivi can sort it out for you."

"Vivi won't have time because she's going back

to work," Cam told him, reaching around his friend to open the front door.

"She's got a new job?" Ryder asked as they left the house and walked in the direction of his massive truck. "Where is she working now?"

"Nowhere, as far as I know. No, she's going to re-open The Rollin' Smoke because that's what she really wants to do. I don't care if it takes fifty years to convince her, but she will resurrect that restaurant. It's her dream, Ryder. I want her to have it."

Ryder nodded and gripped Cam's shoulder. "Good man. But before you broach that subject, tell her you love her and because you love her, you'd do anything for her."

"Point taken."

Ryder surprised him by stepping up and giving him a quick, one-armed hug before slapping him on the back of his head.

Cam glared at him and rubbed the back of his head. "What the hell was that for?"

"For being an idiot." Then Ryder walked around his big truck to the driver's door. He frowned when Cam climbed into the passenger seat. "What the hell are you doing?"

"Hitching a ride." Cam smiled, pulling the door shut. "Vivi will find it difficult to toss me out on my ass when I don't have a car, any access to cash or a phone." Cam grinned. "Just hedging my bets."

Ryder rolled his eyes as he settled in behind the wheel. "I'm not a damn taxi service," he grumbled.

"I know." Cam looked Ryder in the eye. "I'm also relying on you to not let me chicken out at any point between here and her place."

Ryder started the pickup and the engine rumbled. "No problem. I'll just keep slapping some sense into you."

Tough love, Ryder style. Cam smiled, knowing that he wouldn't need it.

He only needed his lover, the love of his life, and his daughter.

Sleep evaded her. It seemed sleep was only something she'd done before her accident and before meeting up with Cam again. So she was awake when she heard pounding on her front door. It was way past ten. Who the hell would be banging on her door at this hour?

Vivi flung back the thin sheet covering her thighs and wondered if it might be another flood warning. Panic caught in her throat and she hurried through her small house to the front door, jerking it open without checking the peephole.

Cam, looking—oh, let's be honest here, simply wonderful—stood on her front porch.

"Check before you open, Viv. I could've been any random dude out to rob or rape you."

Okay, he looked great but his attitude could use some work. "Did you come over here at this crazy hour to harangue me about not taking safety precautions?"

"No, but it's an added bonus," Cam muttered. He pushed a hand through his hair and scowled at her. "Are you going to make me do this outside?"

"Do what?" Vivi asked, confused.

Cam answered her by placing his hands on her hips and pulling her into his hot, strong body, wrapping his arms around her and capturing her mouth in a searing kiss she felt right down to her toes. Her hands found their way to his face—the face she'd missed so much—and she groaned softly. It would be so easy to boost herself up his body, wrap her legs around his hips and allow him to carry her to her bedroom. Judging by his intense kiss and the hardness pushing against her stomach, he'd have no problem with that idea.

One more time, for old times' sake.

And then the pattern would be set. She'd push him away, he'd come back, they'd sleep together, and she'd realize it wasn't enough and she'd end it again. No, she had to be strong and stop this in its tracks.

She didn't want to be strong, though. She wanted to keep kissing Cam under her dull porch light.

Strangely, it was Cam who pulled away, Cam who stopped the craziness. He rested his forehead against hers and sighed. "I see you and my brain shuts down," he said.

Was that a good or bad thing? She had no idea.

"Can we please go inside?" Cam asked her, his sweet breath warm on her face.

Vivi nodded and stepped back into her house.

Cam closed the door behind him and flipped the lock. Vivi shook her head; she lived in a safe neighborhood and she wasn't concerned about crime. But then she remembered that Cam had seen the darker side of life, had rubbed shoulders with some not very nice people, and remained silent.

"How's Clem?" Cam asked, rocking on his heels.

He'd asked her the same question earlier and nothing had changed since then. "She's asleep."

Cam whipped around and walked down her short hallway to Clem's room. Opening her door, Vivi watched as he walked inside to stare down at his daughter. She watched his face soften and his expression turn tender. His love for his daughter was indisputable and Clem was lucky to have such an amazing dad in her life. He'd protect her, love her, tease her and laugh with her. He'd be her first love, her shelter in any storm.

"She's so beautiful, Viv. So amazingly perfect," Cam said, running his finger down Clem's cheek.

She really was. Vivi couldn't help placing her hand on Cam's back and leaning her head against his shoulder. "We did good work," she agreed.

"I want her," Cam said, keeping his voice soft. Then he turned to her and his eyes blazed with conviction, determination sparking in those deep blue depths. "I want you, us. Together. All the time."

Vivi felt her knees soften and gripped the edge of Clem's cot to steady herself. She stared at Cam, not sure whether she'd imagined his softly spoken words. "Sorry?"

Cam's smile was soft and tender. "You heard me, Donner."

"I think I heard you, I'm just not sure I heard you correctly," Vivi replied, idly noticing that her words sounded breathless. Not a surprise, since she was sure that all the air in the room had disappeared.

"Well, let's get out of here and I can say it louder and with more emphasis. As much as I love our daughter, this next conversation is between her momma and me."

Vivi looked at the big hand Cam held out to her, felt her heart pumping and her stomach swooping, the rest of her organs abuzz. Could this be happening? Really? To her? There was only one way to find out. So Vivi placed her hand in his and followed him out of Clem's room. She expected him to turn left to go to her bedroom but instead he turned right and led her into the kitchen, pulling out a chair from under her small wooden dining table. "Sit."

Vivi, for the first time ever, obeyed his order and sat. Mostly because her legs were about to go on strike. Cam moved to stand by the counter, his hands gripping its edge with white fingers. Good, maybe she wasn't the only one who felt off-kilter.

"I'm going to stand here because I've got things that I need to say. It's far easier to kiss you than to talk, so I'm going to keep my hands off you for a few minutes, if that's okay?"

Not really, but if he was about to say what she thought he was about to say, she could live without him touching her, just for a little while. "Okay."

"I was as mad as hell with you for not telling me that I had a child, but I get it now, I do. I'm so glad you put me as your emergency contact, but most of all I'm grateful you didn't drown in that damn flood."

She did, too, but that went without saying.

"I've known you for two weeks and a day, if you count that night we spent together three years ago. My feelings for you should scare me because really, who falls in love in two weeks?"

He was in love with her? Her heart jumped and Vivi tried not to wiggle in her chair as he continued his speech.

"I didn't believe in love, not until you fell back into my life, wet, bedraggled and mud stained." Cam released the counter, flexed his fingers and resumed his hold. "I fought you. I fought what I'm feeling because it scares me stupid. You were right, I did arrange the nannies and the loan as a test. I wanted to prove to myself that you would run, that you are as unreliable as my parents, that you couldn't be trusted.

"I used your hot buttons—your independence and hatred of being controlled—to manipulate the situation to force you out of my life." Cam pulled his bottom lip between his teeth and shook his head. "It was a stupid move, Viv, and I'm so sorry. I will always regret it."

Vivi started to protest that he was being really hard on himself and she'd already forgiven him. But Cam held up his hand, asking for her patience. When she didn't speak, he nodded his thanks.

"But you called me on my BS," he said. "You saw right through me. I should've realized right then that you were right and I was wrong, but I can be a little stubborn."

She couldn't resist a comment. "A little?"

"A lot." His lips kicked up. "Just like you."

Fair.

"So, basically, I'm here to ask you, to beg you, to give me another chance. I can't promise to always agree with you, but I can promise that I will always listen to you. I can't promise to never make a decision on your behalf, but I promise to try and talk everything over with you. I can't promise to change overnight, but I promise to try. If I give you stuff it's to make your life easier, or because I think it'll make you happy, not to control you. I promise to be a better man, Viv, for you and our daughter. And I promise, with my hand on the Bible, that I will be a good dad to Clem."

Of course, he would. She didn't have any doubt about that. Vivi crossed her legs, rested her hands in her lap and cocked her head. She waited a beat and a tense silence filled the room. Cam stood up straighter and she knew that he was wondering whether he was going to be rejected again. She couldn't let him think that, but she had a few things she had to say first. She took a deep breath and tried to smile.

"You're not *that* controlling, Cam. I'm just ultra-sensitive to it because I was controlled and bullied. Sorry to be the one to inform you of this, but I think you are pretty normal for an alpha male with a wide, protective streak. I'm not saying I won't rebel, but I'll try and tone down my instincts. I don't need your money or your gifts. Having you in my life is enough. I absolutely know you will be a good dad to Clem, and our other children, because you are already a good dad."

Was that a glint of moisture she saw in his eyes? Vivi felt her throat tighten and told herself that she couldn't cry. But one tear broke free and then another. She tossed her head and blinked, holding up her hand when Cam stepped her way. "Stay there. Not done."

She wiped away the tears with the balls of her hands, and when she looked at Cam again, she managed a wobbly smile. "One more thing…"

How was she going to say this without bawling? How could she tell him everything that was in her heart, share her deepest conviction? She just had to blurt it out.

"You don't have to be a better man, Cam, because you already are pretty damn spectacular. I am in awe of what you've done, how far you've come. I admire you and respect the hell out of you." Vivi released a wobbly laugh. "I'm so in love with you, McNeal."

"Aw, baby…"

Then Cam was in front of her, lifting her out of her chair and holding her to him. Somehow Vivi found herself in his lap, her fragile wooden chair creaking under their combined weight. The chair could break, the floor could open up and swallow them, and she wouldn't care. Cam was with her and her life finally made sense.

She didn't need him to say the words. He'd shown her that he loved her by opening up, by coming here, by exposing himself. The words would come.

Cam placed his hand on her cheek and tipped her face to look at him. She smiled as she stepped into the happiness that radiated from his eyes. They'd be okay, today, tomorrow, forever. She knew this. She did.

"Vivianne, I didn't want to fall in love or be with anyone. I didn't want to need anyone. I wanted to skim through life. Every rule I made for myself, every promise I made to keep myself apart and safe, I've broken. For you." Cam touched his lips to Vivi's cheek, held himself there. "I love you so damn much."

There. *Finally.* Vivi felt the last ice cube of resistance in her melt, felt herself sink into him. More tears slipped down her face and Cam kissed them away.

"Don't cry. I'm so sorry I hurt you."

Vivi shook her head and wrapped her arms around his neck, burying her face in his strong, warm neck. "Hold me, Cam."

Cam's hands ran up and down her back. "I am. I

will. You're pretty much stuck with me for the next sixty years or so."

Vivi sniffed and then laughed. She pulled her head back to see his tender smile, his soft eyes. "Does that comment come with a ring?"

"Maybe." He rolled his eyes and grinned. "God, who am I kidding? Of course it does, I can't wait to make you my wife." Cam's thumb drifted over her bottom lip. "Can I kiss you now? 'Cause I'm so much better at show than tell."

"I don't know about that. Your tell was pretty damn good. But sure," she said, placing her lips a fraction from his, "kiss away."

"Thank God," Cam muttered before doing exactly that.

And best of all, they got to do all of that and more. Much more. For the rest of the night. And for the rest of their lives.

* * * * *

*What does Angela discover about
Ryder's relationship with her mother
when she visits the ranch?*

Is he telling her the truth?

*Find out in the next installment of
Texas Cattleman's Club: Houston*

Read every scintillating episode!

Hot Texas Nights *by* USA TODAY
bestselling author Janice Maynard

Wild Ride Rancher *by* USA TODAY
bestselling author Maureen Child

That Night in Texas *by Joss Wood*

Rancher in Her Bed *by* USA TODAY
bestselling author Joanne Rock

Married in Name Only *by* USA TODAY
bestselling author Jules Bennett

Off Limits Lovers *by Reese Ryan*

Texas-Sized Scandal *by* USA TODAY
bestselling author Katherine Garbera

Tangled with a Texan *by* USA TODAY
bestselling author Yvonne Lindsay

Hot Holiday Rancher *by* USA TODAY
bestselling author Catherine Mann

It was her first kiss. But that didn't matter.

It was Dane. That was all that mattered. That was all that really mattered.

Dane, the man she'd fantasized about a hundred times—maybe a thousand times—doing this very thing. But this was so much brighter and more vivid than a fantasy could ever be. Color and texture and taste. The rough whiskers on his face, the heat of his breath, the way those big, sure hands cupped her face as his lips moved slowly over hers.

She took a step and the shattered glass crunched beneath her feet, but she didn't care. She didn't care at all. She wanted to breathe in this moment for as long as she could, broken glass be damned. To exist just like this, with his lips against hers, for as long as she possibly could.

She leaned forward, wrapped her fingers around the fabric of his T-shirt and clung to him, holding them both steady, because she was afraid she might fall if she didn't.

Her knees were weak. Like in a book or a movie.

She hadn't known that kissing could really, literally, make your knees weak. Or that touching a man you wanted could make you feel like you were burning up, like you had a fever. Could make you feel hollow and restless and desperate for what came next…

Even if what came next scared her a little.

It was Dane.

She trusted Dane.

With her secrets. With her body.

Dane.

She breathed his name on a whispered sigh as she moved to take their kiss deeper, and found herself being set back, glass crunching beneath her feet yet again.

"I should go," he said, his voice rough.

"No!" The denial burst out of her, and she found herself reaching forward to grab his shirt again. "No," she said again, this time a little less crazy and desperate.

She didn't feel any less crazy and desperate.

"I have to go, Bea."

"You don't. You could stay."

The look he gave her burned her down to the soles of her feet. "I can't."

"If you're worried about… I didn't misunderstand. I mean I know that if you stayed we would…"

"Dammit, Bea," he bit out. "We can't. You know that."

"Why? I'm not stupid. I know you don't want… I don't want…" She stumbled over her words because it all seemed stupid. To say something as inane as she knew they wouldn't get married. Even saying it made her feel like a silly virgin.

She was a virgin. There wasn't really any glossing over that. But she didn't have to seem silly.

She did know, though. For all that everyone saw her as soft and naive, she wasn't. She'd carried a torch for Dane for a long time but she'd also realistically seen how marriage worked. Her brother was a cheater. Her mother was a cheater.

Her father was… She didn't even know.

That was the legacy of love and marriage in her family.

Truly, she didn't want any part of it.

Some companionship, though. Sex. She wanted that. With him. Why couldn't she have that? McKenna made it sound simple, and possible. And Bea wanted it.

Don't miss
Unbroken Cowboy *by Maisey Yates,*
available May 2019 wherever Harlequin® books
and ebooks are sold.

www.Harlequin.com

PHEXPMY0519

SPECIAL EXCERPT FROM

HARLEQUIN®

Desire

*Honorary Westmoreland Thurston "Mac" McRoy
delayed a romantic ranch vacation with his wife for too
long—she went without him! Now it will take all his
skills to rekindle their desire and win back his wife...*

Read on for a sneak peek at
His to Claim
by New York Times *bestselling author Brenda Jackson!*

Thurston McRoy, called Mac by all who knew him, still had
his arms around his mother's shoulders when he felt her tense
up. "Mom? You okay?" he asked, looking down at her.

When his parents glanced over at each other, that uneasy
feeling from earlier crept over him again. Not liking it, he
turned to go down the hall toward his bedroom when his father
reached out to stop him.

"Teri isn't here, Mac."

Mac turned back to his father. His mother had moved to
stand beside his dad.

"It's after two in the morning and tomorrow is a school day
for the girls. So where is she?"

His mother reached out and touched his arm. "She needed
to get away and she asked if we would come keep the girls."

Mac frowned. He knew his wife. She would not have gone
anywhere without their daughters. "What do you mean, she
needed to get away? Why?"

"She's the one who has to tell you that, Thurston. It's not
for us to say."

Mac drew in a deep breath, not understanding any of this. Because his parents were acting so secretive, he felt his confusion and anger escalating. "Fine. Where is she?"

It was his father who spoke. "She left three days ago for the Torchlight Dude Ranch."

Mac's frown deepened. "The Torchlight Dude Ranch? In Wyoming?"

"Yes."

"What the hell did she go there for?"

His father didn't say anything for a minute and then gave Mac an answer. "She said she always wanted to go back there."

Mac rubbed his hand across his face. Yes, Teri had always wanted to go back there, the place he'd taken her on their honeymoon, a little over ten years ago. And he'd always promised to take her back. But between his covert missions and their growing family, there had never been enough time. Teri, who'd been raised on a ranch in Texas, was a cowgirl at heart and had once dreamed of being on the rodeo circuit due to her roping and riding skills. She'd even represented the state of Texas as a rodeo queen years ago.

When they'd married, she had given it all up to travel around the world with her naval husband. She'd said she'd done so gladly. Why in the world would Teri leave their kids and go to a dude ranch by herself?

He knew the only person who could answer that question was Teri.

It was time to go find his wife.

His to Claim
*by New York Times bestselling author Brenda Jackson,
available June 2019 wherever
Harlequin® Desire books and ebooks are sold.*

www.Harlequin.com